"I think it's ridiculous to make us pay our enemies' wages."

"Ridiculous or not, it's what your dad signed up for."

The woman's eyes filled with tears. What had he said? He shuffled his feet and hunched his shoulders as he reviewed his words. He couldn't think of anything that would generate sorrow. The horn blared behind him, and Sid turned and waved at Pete, for the first time relieved to have Pete interrupt him.

"Ma'am? You all right?"

She tipped her chin in the air and blinked rapidly. "Yes. And quit calling me *ma'am*. Anna will do."

Sid grinned as she stalked toward the house. She overflowed with spunk much like his kid sister, Pattie, had before she married that good-for-nothing Peter Tucker, who tried to yell the life out of her. He shook his head and climbed into the truck. He'd return to check on things. He hadn't seen Anna on other trips to the farm. She must work in Grand Island or one of the other larger towns.

He'd try to coordinate one of his trips with a time when she'd be here. He had a feeling Anna was worth getting to know.

CARA C. PUTMAN lives in Indiana with her husband and three children. She's an attorney, a ministry leader and teacher at her church, and lecturer at a Big Ten university. She has loved reading and writing from a young age and now realizes it was all training for writing books. An honors graduate of the University of Nebraska and George Mason University School of Law, Cara loves bringing history to life. She is a regular guest blogger at Generation NeXt Parenting, Keep Me in Suspense, CRAFTIE Ladies of Suspense, and Writer. . .Interrupted and also maintains her own blog, The Law, Books, and Life. If you enjoy *Captive Dreams* (and she really hopes you do!), be sure to read the other books in the series, *Canteen Dreams* and *Sandhill Dreams*. To learn more about her other books and the stories behind the series, be sure to visit her at www.caraputman.com.

Books by Cara C. Putman

HEARTSONG PRESENTS
HP771—Canteen Dreams
HP799—Sandhill Dreams

Captive Dreams

Cara C. Putman

Heartsong Presents

To my mother, Jolene Catlett. Mom, did you have any idea all those days you homeschooled us and drilled grammar into me that someday all that diagramming would pay off in the books I write? Thank you for choosing to invest in us on a daily basis when you could have done any number of other things. I'm a stronger—and smarter—person because of you.

A note from the Author:
I love to hear from my readers! You may correspond with me by writing:

Cara C. Putman
Author Relations
PO Box 721
Uhrichsville, OH 44683

ISBN 978-1-60260-078-2

CAPTIVE DREAMS

All scripture quotations are taken from the King James Version of the Bible.

All of the characters and events in this book are fictitious. Any resemblance to actual persons, living or dead, or to actual events is purely coincidental.

Our mission is to publish and distribute inspirational products offering exceptional value and biblical encouragement to the masses.

PRINTED IN THE U.S.A.

one

May 5, 1944

"Papa, what on earth are those men doing in the fields?"

Anna Goodman swiped her hair from inside her jacket collar as she stared out the window past her father, who sat hunched in his chair. While grief shrouded his eyes and sloped his shoulders, she hated feeling that the burden for the farm outside Holdrege, Nebraska, had transferred to her, a burden she never expected to bear at twenty-one. The men working the fields reclaimed her thoughts. She didn't like the hardness they bore. Nor did she like the idea that German soldiers were the only option. Her spine stiffened until she stood as rigid as a fence post. No matter that the time had come to plant the corn and that the fields around Holdrege hummed with activity. Surely Papa hadn't hired prisoners of war.

Papa buried his head deeper behind the newspaper, huddled in his worn chair in front of the stone fireplace. Anna's heart tightened. She'd been gone only five days, yet he'd aged at least ten years.

"Papa. Look at me. Please." Her words whined until she tightened her lips against more.

The paper rustled, and Anna longed to rip the shield from him. Force him to look at her. Instead, she sighed. His hair might look grayer where it peeked over the paper, but he remained as stubborn as Betsy, the mule he refused to give away.

"Have it your way. I'll find out what they're up to on my own." Anna pulled her jacket tighter and stomped out of the kitchen.

Mama's red-and-white-checked curtains didn't bring a smile

to her face. They were the only cheery thing left in the house now that Mama danced in heaven after a short battle against pneumonia two years earlier. And since the draft board had called his number, her brother, Brent, could no longer fill Papa's silence with his off-the-wall jokes.

Anna stepped outside and wished for the freedom to leave Papa behind his impenetrable wall. He acted like he didn't need her. Reality shouted a different tune in her ears. The inside of the house could only be called a shambles, dirty dishes stacked all over the table and old papers strewn beside his chair where Papa dropped them. Her nose wrinkled at the smell of stale sausage and spoiled food. Papa hadn't even scraped it into the slop pan. The wind stung Anna's cheeks and sucked the air out of her lungs.

The house wasn't the only thing that needed attention. The closer she got to the fields, the more evident it became that they needed care and attention. The rows angled in erratic lines. Weeds sprouted everywhere and, if left unchecked, would choke out the corn as it grew. If only the men in the field didn't have Ps and Ws painted on their clothes. Even if Papa had requested the prisoners, she couldn't imagine the prisoners of war working her land when she came home after a long week at the Kearney airfield.

Her land. Her steps slowed as the words ricocheted around her mind. It had never felt like her land. Indeed, most days it seemed more a ball and chain than a blessing. Yet as the words rolled around, a steady peace filled her chest.

If it was her land, it was high time she treated it that way.

Time to take ownership of it.

If only Papa would.

As her thoughts returned to her papa hiding in the kitchen, she sucked air through her teeth in a whistle. A rush of emotions clambered into the spot that peace had filled.

What are we going to do, Papa? I don't have the energy to shoulder this alone. And you don't have the will. Anna picked up speed and crossed the yard toward the barn.

Beyond the barn, a fence covered in peeling paint with missing boards protected the fields from something, though she'd never known what exactly. Soon deer would leap it with ease to nibble the developing corn plants. It would take weeks, but all too soon the stalks would grow until their tassels touched the sky. Then the hard work started. Anna's shoulders ached thinking about the hours and days she'd spend walking the rows, separating the tassels from the corn. That job made even her sedentary job packing parachutes at the Kearney airfield endurable by comparison.

Anna lifted her face to the sky and released a slow breath. The sun kissed her face with its warmth, and the weariness drained from her. Resolve cloaked her. Whatever the men were doing on the farm, she'd clear it up and get them on their way. She couldn't handle one more challenge at the moment.

She reached the fence and hesitated before climbing the bottom two wooden planks to get a better view of the action. Eight men walked among the rows. Her brow crinkled. The actions of most were unchoreographed and confused. One man strode among the men, pointing and giving instructions as he walked. He spoke to each man in turn and carried an air of assurance. By his uniform, she could tell he was a guard sent with the men, probably a specialist. Yet he acted unlike the other guard, who lounged against a truck.

A prisoner bent toward the ground and ran his fingers through the soil, crumbling it into smaller pieces. He lifted it to his face and inhaled. A smile parted his face from ear to ear, and then he patted the earth back into place and reached with energy for the seed resting at his feet. From her perch, Anna watched as seed corn slipped through his fingers.

"No!" She clenched her teeth as he seemed unable or unwilling to treat the precious seed with care. She'd worked long hours to pay for that corn. "Somebody stop him."

She jumped off the fence and marched toward the man who leaned against the government-issue truck. His uniform hung on him in a rumpled mess. He didn't glance her way, though he had to hear her. She splashed through leftover spring puddles, yet he still ignored her.

"Hey. What are you doing in our fields? They don't know what they're doing. There's seed everywhere." Her anger pushed her voice up an octave, and she struggled to rein in her temper.

The man turned to her. His hat was shoved on top of unruly brown hair that curled slightly around his collar. His shoulders were broad, and she almost stood nose to nose with him.

She stewed as his gaze swept over her body. He leered at her and stood taller. "Calm down, dame."

"I'll calm down when you get these men off my farm. Now."

❧

Her shriek stopped the prisoners in mid-action. Specialist Sid Chance stood and arched his back. Even though he was only twenty-five, he felt the effects of all those hard hits he'd taken during high school football games. He hurried his steps as Pete pushed away from the half tack he'd been lazing against.

"Hey, Pete. What's the problem?"

"Just a broad who don't think we belong here." Pete's Jersey manners and words didn't seem to play well with the woman. Red flamed her tanned cheeks.

Sid shook his head. The little guy seemed to think he stood taller when he ordered everyone around. Only problem was, he couldn't see that the exact opposite occurred.

"Ma'am, I'm Specialist Sid Chance, and this lump of hot air is Private Peter Gurland. What's wrong?"

Her jaw tightened until he wanted to rub his own, ease the tension.

"What's wrong is you. These men. Get off our land now."

Sid turned as Luka, one of the prisoners who enjoyed the outdoor work, approached the group with halting steps.

"Sir, I hate to bother, but men finished."

"You certainly are." The woman stepped closer. "You get these men, these prisoners, off now, before I do something I won't regret."

"Pete, why don't you round them up? Ma'am, how will you plant the corn?"

"I. . .I don't know yet, but I'll come up with something. You must be trespassing, since Papa would never allow them here."

"Mr. Goodman signed a contract for the men, like the other farmers." He took a half step closer to her and cocked his head. "He decided, like most, that the farm needed the extra labor to get the seed in. We're done now, but I'll check back in the next week or so."

"Ya coming, windbag?" Pete's nasally voice jarred his ears.

"Please don't bother. There's been a mistake. We've always handled the farm on our own. We'll do it again." She lowered her gaze and kicked at a clod of dirt. "We can't pay their wages."

"Where else are you going to get farm help? Most of the men are in the military, and everyone else works in industry." He took in her rumpled coveralls. "Like you. We work here at your father's request. Until he informs the camp commander or county agent differently, we'll be back. I always see a job to completion. And you might be surprised about the wages. They aren't as burdensome as you think."

"I think it's ridiculous to make us pay our enemies' wages."

"Ridiculous or not, it's what your dad signed up for."

The woman's eyes filled with tears. What had he said? He shuffled his feet and hunched his shoulders as he reviewed his words. He couldn't think of anything that would generate sorrow. The horn blared behind him, and Sid turned and waved at Pete, for the first time relieved to have Pete interrupt him.

"Ma'am? You all right?"

She tipped her chin in the air and blinked rapidly. "Yes. And quit calling me *ma'am*. Anna will do."

Sid grinned as she stalked toward the house. She overflowed with spunk much like his kid sister, Pattie, had before she married that good-for-nothing Peter Tucker, who tried to yell the life out of her. He shook his head and climbed into the truck. He'd return to check on things. He hadn't seen Anna on other trips to the farm. She must work in Grand Island or one of the other larger towns.

He'd try to coordinate one of his trips with a time when she'd be here. He had a feeling Anna was worth getting to know.

two

Anna's pulse pounded in her ears as she stormed up the weathered stairs to the house. They groaned at her heavy steps. One more thing to add to the long list of items that needed attention. Maybe she should stop caring just as Papa had. He used to take such pride in the appearance of the farm. Or maybe it was Mama who had.

She flung open the screen door and let it slam shut. Papa didn't even shift. She wanted to race to him and scream questions. Why allow help from the very Germans her brother fought? These men, the very sons of the Germans who had held Papa captive during the last war?

He couldn't have invited them. Things weren't that desperate. A Goodman always cares for things on his own. At least that's what he'd always said. Before.

And where would she find the money to pay the wages?

Guilt nibbled at the edges of Anna's thoughts. Her father had ordered her to stay home and abandon her job in Kearney. Yet they needed the cash from her job. The Depression had stripped the family of all but the barest holdings, and the bank accounts had long sat empty of all but the smallest amounts.

The fight left her as she hung up her jacket. She longed to sink to the floor at Papa's feet, place her head in his lap, and feel him stroke her hair like he used to. Instead, she turned on her heel and opened the worn cabinets. Somewhere in here she'd find ingredients for supper.

"Papa, did you collect the eggs today?"

He grunted.

"I'll take that as a no. Fine. I'll be back."

Anna yanked her jacket from its hook by the door and pulled it on. She peeked out the window and felt a pebble lift from her shoulders. The government truck had disappeared, taking the men with it. She slipped out the door and hiked the short distance across the yard to the chicken house. The small wooden structure sagged beneath the weight of its tin roof. The chicken wire kept the chickens in and most of the predators at bay.

"Evening, ladies." Anna waited as the hens clucked and ruffled their feathers. "I hate to intrude, but I need some eggs." Mama had always hummed to the hens to calm them. The more Anna talked to them, the more they danced with jerks. Yet the couple of times she'd remained silent, the chickens had attacked her. One nip at her fingers, and she'd decided to talk when she neared the door.

She cracked the door and slipped into the small space. Her lungs filled with the dust of chicken feed, feathers, and waste. She coughed to clear the air, only inhaling more of the rank odor. *Better make this quick.* She stepped toward the stacked boxes. Reaching under one feathered rump after another, she scooped up the eggs. In less than a minute, she'd filled the bottom of her basket with brown speckled eggs and slid back outside. "See you in the morning."

Indignant cackles were the only reply.

Anna turned away from the door and stopped. She leaned against the building and stared at the display in the sky. Stripes of rich color bled across the creeping darkness. Midnight blue topped lavender that sat on a rich coral. The sun blazed orange as it touched the horizon. Awe filled her at the sight.

"Why do You do it, Lord?" War raged around the globe, yet He took the time to paint the sky each night. She shook her head. Switching the basket to the other hand, she continued to the house.

Silence dominated the dinner of biscuits and scrambled eggs. Her thoughts turned to Specialist Chance and his sympathy. The eggs turned unappetizing at the idea that he saw into places she'd hoped to bury beyond anyone's reach.

With a grunt, Papa shuffled to his room as soon as he'd wiped his plate clean and shoved the last biscuit in his mouth.

"Thank you for the wholesome meal, Anna," she muttered. "So glad you're home." Anna threw her napkin on the table and stood. She busied herself cleaning the kitchen and trying not to wish she'd stayed in Kearney. At least there, her friends wanted to spend time with her.

Reality dictated she didn't have a choice: Each week Papa's physical condition seemed to deteriorate. The scent of alcohol followed him around the house, and his shoulders sloped more—she was sure of it. His eyes were a duller blue. They'd practically faded to gray. She feared they'd soon turn translucent.

He'd stopped living. Somehow, she'd carry on for both of them.

She flipped on the tabletop radio to fill the silence as she brought order to the chaos in the kitchen.

❧

By Sunday, Anna couldn't wait to return to Kearney and her life. Her days might consist of work at the airfield and sleep at the Wisdoms' home, but at least she had a purpose greater than gathering eggs, humoring a cantankerous old man, and milking the cow. She couldn't fight the entrapment that chased her from chore to chore.

Sunday night, Anna planted a kiss on Papa's cheek, relieved her obligations had ended for the week. In an hour, she'd be back in her rented room, ready to return to her job at the airfield. A horn blared outside. Anna startled and grabbed her overnight bag. "See you on Friday, Papa. Don't forget to grab the eggs this week, okay?"

Dottie stood beside her car when Anna skipped down the stairs.

"Way to keep a lady waiting." A large smile creased Dottie's round face. "Let's fly."

Anna opened the passenger door and threw her bag in the footwell. "I'm ready to head back to sanity."

"I don't know if I'd called the Wisdoms sanity or not. Those kids could drive a girl batty, but we'll get you away from your vow of silence."

Anna chuckled. "You have no idea. He seems to get worse each week. I think it's time to get some of his friends involved before he completely disappears."

"Next weekend, darling. Tonight we sail away to a new world. One filled with soldiers, many of them eligible."

"This whole thing is just about finding you a husband."

"Well, if that gets thrown into the mix, I won't complain. I think it's about time I got to use the base chapel for a wedding."

"I want more than a wedding."

Dottie turned and stared. "Haven't you noticed all the eligible men are in uniform? You can work for whatever reason you want. Escaping the farm, your father, whatever. I'm here to find a man who'll take care of me. I won't share a room with you forever."

"Good. You consume more than your share of the dresser, and someday I'll have to do something about that. What a relief if you married first."

Anna ignored Dottie's babble of information about her weekend as the miles flew by. In record time, Dottie pulled the car in front of the Wisdoms' Victorian. The home over-flowed with people. Between the five Wisdoms and six boarders, every spare nook and cranny was filled. The housing shortage caused by those working the airfield made Anna grateful for any bed. Maybe she should be thankful for the quiet on the farm each weekend, but Papa made it hard.

She stumbled up the steps and through the front door Dottie propped open. The sounds of two boys fighting in the parlor assaulted her. Anna tossed her bag on the polished wooden steps, ignored the boys, and turned to follow the scent of spiced cider into the kitchen.

"Here. Let me grab your bag for you. I'd love to schlep it up to our room—no tip required."

"Thanks, Dottie." Anna turned back and caught the grimace

on Dottie's face. She ran her fingers along the smooth chair rail as she continued down the hall. "Good evening, Mrs. Wisdom."

"Hello, dear. How was your weekend?" Bonnie Wisdom turned from the pot she stirred on the stove. Her turquoise eyes studied Anna with care as silence settled between them. "That good? I'm sorry."

"Maybe someday I'll enjoy trips home. Until then, I'll work hard during the week and endure days on the farm. Life and fun used to fill the place. That hasn't been the case for a long time."

"Grief takes time to fade, Anna."

"Isn't two years enough?"

"There's no magic time. Some people move on quickly; others linger with the one who has passed." Mrs. Wisdom settled at the table next to Anna. "Do you think you should go home?"

"I can't do that. It's too hard." A lump filled her throat. Anna sagged in her seat and played with the edge of the tablecloth. She willed her eyes not to fill with tears and winced when one escaped. "I've lost everybody dear to me."

"You have." Mrs. Wisdom turned down the flame under the pot, filled a mug with cider, and joined her at the table. She reached across the cloth and handed Anna a cup. "But you have time to reach your father. And your brother may still come home. Until then, we must ask God to protect them and bring them safely home."

As Mrs. Wisdom prayed aloud, Anna bowed her head and tried to join in. The only words that filled her prayer begged for her faith to be restored before it disappeared with her hope.

three

Reveille echoed through the air. Sid pulled the scratchy wool blanket over his head before facing the inevitable. The army waited for no man, no matter how tired or what dreams haunted his sleep. He wanted to return to the image of a petite blond dynamo in his dreams. Instead, bleary-eyed, he stumbled onto the floor and into the chest at the foot of the bed. A howling wind had chilled the air in the barracks overnight to the point that even the three coal stoves placed down the middle of the large room couldn't heat it. Through his socks, the concrete floor felt like ice.

He opened the box's lid and grabbed a fresh uniform before heading to the washroom. In minutes, he dashed out the door and across the compound to the mess hall. His stomach growled as soon as he opened the door and the smell of powdered eggs scrambled in bacon grease reached his nose.

"Sounds like you need to cut to the front of the line."

"Thank you, sir. I mean, no, sir." Sid's words tangled to a halt when he realized his commanding officer spoke to him. "I'll be fine, Colonel Smith." He never used to be tongue-tied. Now anytime he saw his CO, he remembered the fiasco at Fort Robinson. He wanted to slam a hand over his mouth before more inane words escaped.

Colonel Smith nodded and proceeded through the line. Sid groaned.

"Sound like an officer in training. 'Yes, sir. No, sir. Right away, sir.'" Larry Heglin sneered as he shouldered past Sid into the chow line.

Times like this, it was hard for Sid to turn his cheek and walk away. It would be so much easier to put a guy like

16

Heglin in his place. The private second class despised him. Sid slouched and screwed his eyes shut.

"Wakey, wakey, bud."

Sid opened his eyes as the scent of coffee swirled beneath his nose. Trent Franklin stood in front of him, sipping a cup of coffee while offering another to Sid.

"Thanks." Sid accepted the cup and yelped when the hot liquid scalded his lips. He touched the tender spot with his free hand. "This should come with a warning. So what's today's agenda?"

"First, get some food. Then back to the prisoners' side of camp. I don't think any groups are heading to farms today." Trent grabbed a tray. Throwing a fork and knife on it, he slid into the line.

"Nothing like passing time in a guard shack."

"Yep. Another exciting day."

Sid stepped up to the line and waited as soldiers slopped food onto his plate at each station. His mind wandered to the spitfire he'd met at the Goodman farm. She returned to his thoughts without invitation. Something about her intensity and emotion had caught his attention. Something the other gals he knew failed to do. Something had caused all that emotion, and he wanted to learn what. He also wondered what she was like on a routine day when fatigue didn't pull her down. If her smile could match the fire that danced in her eyes.

"Hey. You still with me?"

"Yep."

"Sure you are. Maybe I should replace you next time you head to the Goodman farm."

"Why would you do a crazy thing like that? It's just another farm."

"Your mind's lived somewhere else since you got back. You didn't even join us at the USO this weekend."

Sid shouldered Trent. "A guy needs an occasional break."

"From good times?" Trent shook his head and pushed

through the tables to a vacant one. "You'll come back. This war could last for years. You like the girls too much to stay away."

Sid slid into a seat. Unease settled over him. He'd always liked his life, but something had changed. Maybe he wasn't as content as he thought.

Trent's prediction came true. The day dragged as Sid sat in a guard tower. In an effort to pass the time, he fiddled with a broken searchlight. The bulb had shattered inside the fixture, and he had to pull the glass and metal out piece by piece. The task took time, but not nearly enough to fill even the morning.

Once the light worked again, he paced the rim of the tower. His gaze swept across the camp. Camp Atlanta housed about nineteen hundred prisoners of war at any given time. A small town had sprung from the fields to support the camp, administrative buildings, and soldiers' quarters.

Row after orderly row of twenty-by-one-hundred-feet frame buildings spaced thirty feet apart spread across the camp. Barbed wire fences surrounded the prisoners' section, clearly delineating the line between compounds. He looked over the eleven buildings that formed the hospital complex, then to the administration buildings and bakery. Small groups of prisoners, guards, and soldiers circulated around the camp, but nothing unusual happened.

A stiff breeze snaked past Sid's jacket collar and down his neck. The sun had dived behind a cloud, taking the warmth with it. With a shudder, he walked back inside the tower. The glass windows didn't provide enough protection from the Nebraska weather but were better than the alternative.

Trent huddled over a cup of coffee. "Seen enough?"

"Yep. There's so much to see today. The dead wire's where it's always been. The prisoners are still glad to be here and not in the war. And we're bored as usual." Sid leaned against the doorframe.

"Isn't this why we enlisted? See the world—or Nebraska. I'm sure that was in the army's materials."

Sid shook his head. "I don't mind Nebraska so much." Between Forts Robinson and Atlanta, he'd seen more of Nebraska than he'd intended. Europe had been a little more what he had in mind. He'd hoped to serve with Patton or someone equally brilliant rather than work as military police at a home-front base. "At least the people are friendly."

"Yep." A goofy grin stretched Trent's face. "You should have joined me. The gals were extra friendly this weekend."

Sid studied Trent, not sure he wanted to dive too deeply into what Trent meant. "How about the base theater? What's showing?"

"Doesn't matter—you'll come whether it's John Wayne or Laurel and Hardy."

A siren pealed across the camp. Sid rushed outside to the platform. "Man the gun, Trent. Let's see what's going on."

The phone inside the guard shack rang. Sid turned to see Trent grab it with one hand while keeping the other firmly on the gun's handle. Trent would let him know what was going on as soon as he knew anything, so Sid turned back to the prisoners' section. No matter where he looked, nothing appeared out of place. The prisoners outside had frozen in their spot, probably too scared to move. He looked around the dead man's line. As far as he could tell, no one had strayed there. He reached for his riot gun just in case he'd missed something in one of the blind spots behind the buildings.

Other soldiers rushed toward the compound, guns at the ready. Sid prayed no one pulled a trigger unnecessarily. The last thing he wanted to witness was the slaughter of unarmed men. To date, nothing like that had happened at Camp Atlanta. He didn't want today to be the first time. Especially not when he and a small unit of men manned the guard towers.

The window rattled behind him, and Sid whipped toward it, his glance darting between the guard tower and the perimeter.

Travis gave him the OK sign and motioned him in.

Sid reentered the small tower. "What was that all about?"

"Someone leaned on the siren by mistake."

"Sure. It's so easy to hit the button on top of the machine, and so hard to find the button to turn it off." Sid made a mental note to find out who it was and give him a talk that would ensure he'd never be so careless again.

"Maybe we aren't the only ones bored today."

"Right. Here's hoping they punish the fool."

"Don't forget, you get to be a part of that with your new duties, Chance."

Sid nodded. His new duties as a specialist would take awhile to get used to, but he'd enjoy this one.

Things settled down in the compound. Sid's thoughts wandered as he watched nothing happen. In the coming days, he'd escort prisoners to local farms where they could fill the desperate need for farm labor. He stifled a groan at the long days filled with nothing to do. The prisoners didn't want to escape. And he didn't sign up to be a taxi driver for PWs. The only variety in his days came from locals who decided they didn't want the Germans around, after all. Like one particular blond.

Maybe he should stop by the Goodman farm, make sure everything was okay. Maybe find out how to contact her. He didn't want to rely on stopping by. And it wouldn't hurt if he could get a better sense of the underlying story. As he closed his eyes, he knew he would.

He would do anything to bring a smile to Miss Goodman's face.

four

May 12, 1944

Friday afternoon, Anna glanced back at the Wisdoms' home before inching inside Dottie's car. She tossed her bag into the backseat and collapsed next to her friend.

"Ready for another weekend?" Dottie's grin tipped to one side.

"At home? Have I ever been?" Anna flipped her bobbed blond curls behind her ears. "I wonder what crisis Papa will create this weekend."

"He only wants to keep you home."

Anna stared out the window and watched Kearney slip behind them. Part of her understood that was what Papa wanted. Her at home. All the time. But the thought of staying in that too-quiet farmhouse pulled the air from her lungs. And they couldn't sacrifice her income, could they? Without it, there was far too little money on the farm. Much as Papa might want to avoid the reality, cash remained a necessity.

So she'd balance her job at the factory with her help at the farm—though the image of the crooked rows of corn made her wonder if twenty-four hours a day, each day of the week, would be enough time. Too much work existed for two people who gave their all, let alone two fragmented people.

She had to pull Papa out of his depression. Keep him out of the bottles that had turned into his only friends. Somehow. The miles rolled by in silence as Anna's thoughts flitted from idea to idea.

Dottie turned the car off the highway and onto the rutted driveway leading to the farm long before Anna had a plan or felt ready. Dottie turned toward Anna. "You know how to

21

reach me if you need anything."

"Thanks." The town girl forgot that to reach her, Anna had to walk to the neighbor's farm to use the phone. "See you Sunday."

"Yes, ma'am."

Anna grabbed her bag and slipped from the car. The house looked desolate with no light shining from a single window. She squared her shoulders and marched to the door. Ready or not, another weekend awaited her.

"Who's there?" Papa stumbled through the kitchen. "Annie, that you?"

"Yes, Papa. I'm home."

"Harrumph. About time. I'm tired of eating scrambled eggs three meals a day. The chores need you, too."

Welcome home. Anna stilled the words that wanted to explode from her mouth. Every lesson she'd ever heard about honoring her parents raced through her mind. She unclenched her hands and forced a smile on her lips. "Let me drop my bag. Then I'll get started."

He grunted and turned back to the living room and his chair.

Anna threw her bag on her bed and sank onto it. The twin frame creaked in protest. She held her head in her hands. She'd spent the week working full days at the airfield, sewing and packing parachutes and patching airplane wings. Long, twelve-hour days. Exhaustion tempted her to lie down. Rest for just a moment. But if she allowed herself to relax, she doubted she'd get up before morning. Then what would the poor cow do as her udder threatened to explode?

With a groan, Anna pulled herself off the bed and pasted a smile on her face.

"Anna?" Papa's voice bellowed down the hallway. "Where'd you go, girl? Time's wasting. Where's my dinner?"

She headed toward his voice, the knot in her stomach tightening. She had to survive the weekend. . .somehow. She'd make sure there was a farm left for Brent to come home to if it killed her. As Papa continued to yell, she braced against the thought that it might.

❧

Sid shrugged out of his jacket, keeping one hand on the wheel, and threw it on the truck seat next to him. The truck jostled around a large pothole as he traveled the back highway toward the Goodman farm. The week had been jammed with activity. He hadn't swung by and checked on the fields as promised. That inability to follow through grated on him. The moment his duties ended Friday afternoon, he'd known exactly where he needed to go.

Now he neared the farm. Compared to the other fields lining the county roads, Goodman's acres showed neglect. Enough neglect to make him wonder how on earth the spitfire from last week thought she could handle the acres alone.

Maybe Anna had a hidden solution, but he doubted it.

The image of Mr. Goodman's face flashed through Sid's mind. He'd only interacted with the man once, but his features had been twisted into a mask of bitterness. The man had argued with the county extension agent in charge of assigning prisoners to work groups that he must have help. No one had stuck around on the farm, and he couldn't maintain the three hundred acres on his own. Sid had hustled his team to the farm, only to have Mr. Goodman refuse to open his door or leave his house.

The man seemed filled with contradictions. Arguing passionately for help one day and ignoring the same the next.

Sid pulled down the narrow lane that led to the farmhouse and barn. If Anna had come home tonight, her sharp tongue would make his visit interesting. He'd been serious when he told her he'd keep an eye on the place. Someone needed to. She reminded him so much of his sister, Pattie, before she married Peter. The similarities hurt.

He stopped the truck in front of the barn, walked to the house, and banged on the back door. A shuffling sound neared the door. The curtain on the window swept to the side, and then Mr. Goodman opened the door a crack and peered out.

"What you need, boy?" The hint of something sour carried on his breath.

"Wanted you to know I'm here checking the fields."

"Why waste your time?" Mr. Goodman's face twisted.

"The army intends to fulfill its contract with you." Sid tried to peer around him to see if Anna had made it home. He stepped back when it became clear Mr. Goodman wouldn't invite him in. "Good night."

The door slammed in his face. "All right." Sid spun on his heel. He walked to the edge of the nearest field and started to cut through it. The sound of a booming voice carrying on the wind halted his progress. He strained to hear the words.

"Girl, you're one to sass me. Home an hour, and I get nothing but disrespect. Get over here and clean up this mess."

The words tapered off, and Sid hesitated. The cause of the yelling wasn't his business. Maybe the man lived life angry. That would explain why everyone had left. Which developed first? The leaving, the anger, or the drinking?

The thought of his brother-in-law and the way he harangued Pattie left Sid's blood boiling. He couldn't protect Pattie across the miles, but he refused to let anyone treat another woman that way. He started across the yard to the house.

A door slammed shut. Anna stumbled from the farm house, muttering under her breath. Her head was down, shoulders hunched as if protecting herself from the next shell her father would lob.

She scooped up a bucket where it listed against the side of the house and hurried toward the barn. Headed to chores? Her face looked pale with splotches of color on her cheeks. He followed in case she needed help. Though he could imagine her response. He surveyed the fields. There wasn't much he could do about them until he returned with his group of PWs.

Anna disappeared around the corner of the barn, and he picked up his pace. A small shack stood tucked in the shadow of the barn. The cacophony coming from the ramshackle hut indicated it was a chicken coop. Her steps slowed as she neared the door then slipped inside.

Five minutes later, Sid lounged against the side of the barn when she stepped outside. "Need help with the chores?"

She startled and juggled the basket, mouth open as she stared at him. "What are you doing here?"

A lazy grin creased his face. "I told you I'd keep an eye on the farm. I keep my promises."

"We can't pay. Anything."

"The United States Army takes care of my pay, ma'am."

The tightness around her eyes eased, and the redness in her eyes almost disappeared as she gave a silent laugh. "So they do. But I imagine you have other tasks than keeping an eye on a failing farm."

"Not once my prisoners are assigned." He reached for the basket, and their fingers brushed. Electricity flowed between them, and he swallowed hard. "Let me help you with that; then we can get to anything else that needs to be done."

She chewed on her lower lip as her glance darted toward the house and then around the yard. She seemed determined to look anywhere but at him. Finally, her gaze landed on him, and she squared her shoulders as if reaching a decision. "I'd like that, but only if you quit calling me *ma'am*."

He dipped his head. "All right." He considered her a moment. "Who does the work when you aren't here?"

"I don't know. Papa must drag himself out of the house most days. But sometimes when I get here, the poor cow looks so miserable I wonder when he milked her last." She pushed a blond curl behind her ear, but it refused to stay in place. His fingers itched to reach out and brush it back. "He milks and does the other chores when he gets thirsty or hungry. He wasn't always like this. But now he's unbearable. I dread coming home, but I have to or there won't be anything for my brother to return to when this war finally ends." Her hand covered her mouth as if to stop more words from escaping.

Sid slipped his hands into his pockets and rocked back on his heels. "Look. Instead of standing here in the yard, let me take you to dinner. Give you a break for a bit." Her forehead crinkled as she frowned at him. "Think of it as a chance to educate me about the farm. What works best. What to avoid. Between us, we'll keep the farm running."

She opened her mouth then closed it. "There's a lot to do, and I only have until Sunday."

"All the more reason to accept my offer. And give me some way to contact you during the week if I have a question." He quirked an eyebrow at her in his best Clark Gable impression and waited.

"What's keeping you, girl? I'm starving in here." The angry words carried from the house to their position. Anna squared her shoulders and set her chin.

"I accept. But on one condition."

"What?"

"You milk the cow while I make a quick supper for Papa. I need to know he gets at least three days of good meals a week." She hurried toward the house before he could stop her or claim that contact information.

He entered the shadowy interior of the barn and waited for his eyes to adjust. He eased down the aisle toward the cow standing in her pen. He stared at the large animal, then swallowed when he spied her bulging udder. Was now a good time to mention he didn't know the first thing about milking a cow? Guess he'd learn the old-fashioned way, good ol' trial and error. If he was lucky, he might finish before Anna joined him.

He grabbed the pail that rested on the rail and eased into the stall. The cow stamped her feet impatiently and kept her eyes on him.

Then again, he might be branded by the cow's hoof.

five

The sound of Nellie pounding the stall with her hooves sent Anna running back into the barn. All thoughts of fixing a meal for Papa disappeared with the image of Nellie kicking Sid. She turned the corner and found Sid cowering in the stall as far from Nellie as he could get. The docile cow had backed him into the corner. Her hind feet tap-danced while her tail twitched his side like a switch. He clutched the milk bucket in his hand and grimaced when he caught her watching.

Anna tried to wipe all expression from her face as she eased into the stall.

"Here, Nellie. That's a good girl."

Nellie approached her, freeing Sid.

"You can come out of the corner now."

Sid hurried around the edge of the stall until he stood next to Anna. "You didn't warn me she's violent."

"Oh, she's not. You must have riled her. What did you do?"

Color flushed Sid's cheeks, and Anna wondered if she'd somehow pushed too far. "I'll have you know I didn't do anything. Just sat down and started pulling on those. . .things. . . trying to get the milk to come."

"You haven't milked before?" Anna laughed at his expression. "Here, stand next to me, and I'll show you how. Next time she won't back you into the corner." He settled behind her while she explained milking as she stripped Nellie dry. The cow mooed in relief, and as the bucket filled, Anna could understand why. Papa simply wasn't getting the poor cow milked often enough. Keep that up, and her milk might dry up.

Once the pail was filled and covered, Sid carried it to the porch. He stared at Anna as she paused with her hand on the door. "Still want to have dinner with me?"

Anna looked at the house. Anything sounded better than going inside. "I still have to get Papa supper. I'll fix him a quick sandwich, and then we can leave." She made the food then followed Sid to the truck. They stopped at a diner, but the meal passed full of awkward pauses. He asked questions about the farm interspersed with requests for her phone number. She finally gave it to him to end that conversation thread. The more questions he asked about the farm, the more she revealed how much she didn't know.

"I don't want to talk about the farm anymore."

"Why? Afraid you'll find something I know more about than you do?"

She sat, arms crossed, staring at him. "Why did you decide to be mean?"

"You put me in a stall with a crazy cow."

"She's sweet. You didn't know what to do with her."

Sid shrugged. "And your dad doesn't have a problem with alcohol."

Her mouth dropped open as her eyes widened. "What did you say?"

"He stumbles around and always has the telltale smell on his breath, or aren't you home often enough to notice?"

"He does not have a problem with alcohol." She pulled her napkin from her lap and threw it on the table. Even if he did, that was her responsibility. She didn't need some soldier to act better than she because of Papa's struggles. "I'm ready to go home."

"Fine." Sid stalked to the counter to pay. The drive home passed in terrible silence.

&

All week, Anna couldn't get their argument out of her mind. Why should she care what he thought? She'd hardly known him a week. By Wednesday morning, she tried to force her thoughts to anything but Sid Chance as the bus rattled to a stop outside the gated entrance to the Kearney Army Air

Field. Each time she passed the guardhouse, Anna thought one good puff from the big bad wolf or other enemy would blow the structure over, removing any deterrent to entering the complex. If the Germans ever made it to Nebraska, the guard shack certainly wouldn't stop them.

Why couldn't she get that obnoxious soldier out of her mind?

A soldier waved the bus through, and Anna stifled a yawn. Ever since her weekend home, she'd struggled to regain her normal routine in Kearney. This morning, she'd met the bus on time only because Dottie had prodded her.

Normally, returning to the routine wasn't a problem. The hard work on the farm filled her days at home as her job at the factory filled her days in Kearney. Her evenings passed in slow minutes in the Wisdoms' parlor with the other boarders. This week, though, the Wisdoms' youngest son, Andy, came down with something and barked through the nights. It seemed as though his bed stood next to hers separated by only a paper-thin wall. No matter how she tossed and turned, Anna couldn't block out his coughs. And Sid invaded the dreams that peppered her erratic sleep.

A shadow of helplessness followed her steps. The intricacies of farming eluded her. Papa had trained Brent on those, fully intending him to be his partner. A sigh escaped at the thought of Brent so far away when he should be here. If he were, life and Papa could return to normal.

"Earth to Anna." Dottie pinched Anna's shoulder.

"Ouch. What was that for?"

"You were somewhere far away. Didn't want you to miss our stop."

The driver ground the bus's gears as the bus chugged to a stop in front of the warehouse that housed the parachute packers. Anna rubbed the sore spot and frowned. "I can think of less painful ways to catch my attention."

"Sure, but not nearly as fun."

"You and your warped sense of fun."

Dottie grinned and grabbed her purse. "Spend a day with my family, and you'll understand." She stood and inched her way down the aisle. "Come on, slowpoke. Time to get to work saving all our airmen."

Dottie's flippant tone grated. Anna prayed over each parachute, asking God to protect the man assigned to it. Invariably, Brent invaded those prayers. He piloted a B-17 like the ones processed at Kearney. The big bombers served as a daily reminder of the danger he flew into with each mission.

"Wow, you're even more morose. Don't worry about him." Dottie linked arms with Anna as they walked to the warehouse. "Brent's fine."

Dottie knew her too well after rooming together for a year. Anna worried her bottom lip between her teeth. "We haven't received a letter in weeks."

"That you know of."

"True." Surely Papa hadn't forgotten to show her any of Brent's letters. "No letters must mean everything's okay. That he's busy. But. . ." The word trailed off as her mind filled in all kinds of alternatives.

"Let's focus on what we can do. And that's pack these parachutes so the boys are as safe as we can make them."

Anna stashed her lunch bag and jacket into the locker next to Dottie's. Time to focus on what mattered right now. That meant doing her job thoroughly and with attention. One mistake could have far-reaching consequences she didn't want to consider.

The day eased by, and Anna fought to stay focused on the intricate pattern she folded into the silk. Some days the work felt mindless, perfect for pondering other issues. Today that mindlessness propelled her thoughts back to the farm.

Somehow she had to figure out a schedule for cultivating the crops. They couldn't afford another off year. She couldn't imagine paying the mortgage and taxes plus surviving on what she made at the base. A solution existed. Somewhere. Maybe some of the men from church would help. If she could only get Papa to join her, she knew they'd ease him from his cave.

"Miss Goodman."

Anna's head snapped up as Corporal Robertson's voice sounded close to her ear.

"Yes, sir?"

"You haven't moved in fifteen minutes. Are you feeling well? Or do you think the war is in hand and we no longer need to work hard to stay ahead of Hitler?"

Anna opened her mouth, thoughts flying through her head. She caught Dottie's grimace and counted to five instead. "I'm sorry, sir. I didn't realize I'd stopped."

"See that you work. Too many men depend on the job you do."

He stalked the rows of women, and Anna relaxed as he diverted his attention to other unfortunate gals.

"Have you heard from Specialist Chance?" Dottie leaned toward her with an eager light in her eyes.

"No. You'd know if I had. Goodness, you're my roommate and best friend."

"I hoped I'd missed a note or a call. He's so good-looking."

Anna rolled her eyes. "You need a new pair of glasses." Sure, he was nice enough, but she'd always gone for tall blonds. Sid was average height with dark hair creeping out from under his cap. She fully expected that the next time she saw him, if there was a next time, some army barber would have shorn his hair back to the scalp again.

"Looks are fine, but there's something deeper in him, too."

"Now wait a minute, Dottie. When have you seen him?"

Dottie blushed and looked down at the silk overflowing her lap. "I may have bumped into him at a USO dance or two."

"And you never introduced us?"

"Why would I do that? Besides, you aren't interested, remember?" Dottie's grin telegraphed that she saw through Anna's protests.

Anna clamped her mouth shut before she said anything she might not regret but should. One thing about having a best friend: She sure knew how to dive under the layers of protection Anna had developed. Was she jealous? Sid was a nice man, but he certainly hadn't done anything to indicate he was interested in her in more than a helpful manner. And they hadn't parted on good terms.

Whether she wanted to admit it, she needed his help. The farm needed the prisoners' labor to survive.

She'd simply stop spending anything beyond the bare necessities so she could pay the prisoners. Pressure built behind her eyes at the thought. That money should pay taxes, but without crops, there'd be no reason to pay. If only she could delay payment. What had Papa been thinking? They didn't have the money, and they didn't have a way to transport the prisoners.

Her stomach tightened at the thought of prisoners on the farm. Papa could take care of himself. But Germans on the farm felt unsafe. It felt like bringing the war squarely to their corner of Nebraska. Not just this war, but the Great War, too. The fact remained that no other source of labor existed. Not while most young men wore uniforms, and all other able bodies worked in the war industry.

Maybe a neighbor could loan a couple of prisoners to work her farm every other day for a while. If two men worked the fields consistently, the money might stretch to pay the forty-cent-an-hour wage. She'd have to play with the numbers and cut back her expenses, but it might be enough to turn the farm around. A couple of prisoners more often wouldn't cost as much as a large group once a week. And the results might be better.

A spark of hope warmed her. She'd have to talk to Papa, but maybe she could pull this off and save the farm, after all. Even if it required working with Specialist Chance.

six

Silence filled the truck as the three men jostled against each other. Sid had transported prisoners to the Goodman farm all week. The prisoners rocked with the jouncing of the truck, serious expressions painted on their faces. Franz usually loved the chance to leave camp and into the open air for a day. Instead, today he sat slumped in the seat, the brim of his hat pulled over his eyes. Next to him sat Otto, his back ramrod straight as if condemned to a firing squad. Five other prisoners jostled around the bed of the truck. He'd drop them off at a neighboring farm after Franz and Otto were settled at the Goodmans'.

"All right. Someone explain the long faces."

Both looked straight ahead. Franz's Adam's apple bobbed up and down as he swallowed. Hard.

"Either of you sick?"

More silence.

"Unable to work?"

Their stoic looks didn't falter.

"Fine. I'll drop you last and get to the bottom of this after the others are settled at the Berkeley place. If you lose time, it's not my fault."

Otto looked at him quickly then glanced back to the road. "We not like the man."

"Shh." Franz nudged Otto into the door.

Sid looked at them then back at the road. "Which man? Mr. Goodman?"

Franz's chin dropped in a quick nod. "It true."

"Why? There has to be a reason."

"He yells when we there. Blames us for. . ." Franz whirled a finger in the air as if trying to find the right word. He shrugged. "He not nice. Not like you."

"His farm needs the labor, and you two are the perfect fit. This will be where you work three days a week. More as we get closer to harvest or detasseling."

"Not mind hard work." Otto rubbed his hands together and then held them to his nose and inhaled. "I love land. Much better than battle."

Franz nodded.

"If there's a problem, let me know. I'll take care of it."

The men nodded, but the looks on their faces made Sid wonder if they'd follow through.

The program of prisoners helping as labor on farms remained new. Some counties and communities had embraced the program as the answer to the severe labor shortage. Other farmers and towns resisted the idea of having the "enemy" on their farms. After Anna's reaction that first time, it didn't surprise Sid that Mr. Goodman fell in the latter category.

That didn't change reality. He needed the help. Especially if he wanted to keep the farm a going concern until his son returned.

Sid dropped off Franz and Otto before continuing up the road. The two trudged toward the barn as if to a torture chamber. Sid continued to the Berkeleys'. Unlike their reticent neighbor, this family embraced the extra help. He often had to turn away as they invited the prisoners to the house to eat lunch in violation of the rules. He wished more families treated the prisoners like men and valued human beings; it would do more to end the threat of future misunderstandings and wars between the countries than anything else.

The prisoners jumped out of the truck as soon as it pulled into the Berkeleys' farm and hurried to the barn. Sid waited until he caught Tom Berkeley's eye. "I'll be back to get these men around four thirty. That okay?"

"Sure. I can keep them plenty busy until then."

"All right. Let me know if there are any problems."

Tom patted the shotgun that leaned next to him against his

rusted pickup. "We've got it covered. I don't expect trouble."

Sid turned the truck around and headed toward the Goodmans'.

Before he saw the house at the end of the lane, Sid heard screams. Instead of slowing the truck down, he whipped it next to the barn and braked hard. The motor coughed and went silent.

A bird sang its song somewhere nearby, but otherwise a cast of silence covered the farm. What had happened to the yelling he'd heard?

Sid scanned the distance between the house and barn but saw nothing unusual. Might as well check on Mr. Goodman first. He climbed the steps to the porch and pounded on the door. "Mr. Goodman?" He waited a moment but heard no answering call or footsteps. "Mr. Goodman, Specialist Chase here. Everything okay?"

It felt strange yelling at the man through the door. As he knocked again, the door creaked open. Sid slipped inside.

"Is that one of you Krauts?" The slurred words filtered from a room behind the kitchen. "Show yourselves, cowards. Couldn't even fight like men, could you? Had to go and get captured. No wonder we beat you in the last war."

The words trailed off, followed quickly by what sounded like a snore. Sid eased down the hallway, checking the rooms he passed. The kitchen and living area stood empty. When he reached the first bedroom, he found Mr. Goodman slouched over in a chair, an empty bottle of liquor next to him. Sid checked to make sure he still breathed before rousing him.

"Let's get you to bed."

Mr. Goodman mumbled something but staggered beside Sid as he led the man to the double bed. Once the man lay safely on the bed, Sid stepped back and watched him awhile. How often did Mr. Goodman allow himself to descend into a drunken stupor like this? If frequently, no wonder the farm was in its current state. And if Mr. Goodman yelled consistently, Sid understood why Franz and Otto cowered at the thought of working here.

Something had to be done, but what? He wouldn't fail Anna like he'd failed Pattie.

❧

The week passed quietly for Anna. Days filled with work followed by nights at the Wisdoms'. Some nights, everyone gathered around the cleared dining-room table to play games. Other nights, Anna escaped to her room. Until Dottie slipped in, she'd have a few minutes to escape and pretend the war had ended and life had somehow returned to normal.

On Wednesday afternoon, as Anna sat in the hangar patching the silk wings on a plane, the thought of normalcy made her snort. It felt like decades since the four of them had eked out a living on the farm. That time had required hard work, too, but it hadn't seemed as daunting when they would all gather around the dinner table at the end of a long day.

Now Mama was gone, Sid accused Papa of having a drinking problem, and Brent fought somewhere in Europe. There was nothing she could do about Brent, and Papa was a puzzle. She longed to help him but didn't know how. She ran her thumbs over the pads of her fingers and winced at the thick calluses. Life had certainly changed. Anna dropped her needle and rubbed her hands up and down her arms against the sudden chill that engulfed her.

A bell sounded, startling her from her thoughts.

"Lunchtime. Come on, Anna." Dottie bounced from her seat and pulled Anna with her. "I think Mrs. Wisdom sent us sandwiches and fruit."

"She usually does."

"But today's might have real meat."

"Not a fan of Spam?"

"Think positively with me." Dottie's bright smile coaxed an answering one from Anna. "Maybe there's pheasant tucked between the bread."

"In May?"

"So? Nothing wrong with wishful thinking."

"You take it to an extreme, but I like the thought." Anna grabbed her lunch from her locker and followed Dottie into the lunchroom. Heat brushed over her as she passed the cafeteria line. Her nose wrinkled at the stale aroma of overcooked hamburger surprise. "Let's find a table far away, okay?"

Dottie looked at her, concern filling her eyes. "You feeling all right?"

"I will once we eat."

Once they seated themselves at a small table, Dottie announced, "This week let's do something different. You work too hard, and I have a remedy."

Anna stilled, her unwrapped sandwich partway to her mouth. This should be interesting.

"The USO's holding a dance tomorrow night. We haven't gone in a long time. It would be good for both of us." A knowing grin creased her face as if she'd uncovered a winning argument. "It's our patriotic duty, you know. Spend time with the boys before they ship out. What does it hurt to forget about things like farm responsibilities for a while? What do you say?"

"Tomorrow night?"

"Right. I'll even get you back to that prison of a farm on Friday. You can still be the ultra-responsible daughter."

The idea actually sounded fun. Anna wouldn't mind an evening with the soldiers. Most were nice and wanted someone to spend a few minutes with while they talked about their girls back home. Sure, some prowled for prospects, but she easily spotted them.

"I guess it is my civic duty." Anna laughed at the thought. "Imagine Papa's reaction to that argument."

"Who cares? We'll put a spring in your step before you retreat to the farm."

⁂

Thursday night, Anna prepared with care. It felt good to spend time playing up her curls rather than pulling her hair out of her face. And she felt downright feminine putting on a dress that swirled around her knees rather than wearing work clothes. Dottie was right. Too much time had passed since she'd relaxed and had some fun. She touched up her crimson lipstick then followed a giddy Dottie to her car.

As soon as they pulled into the USO parking lot, the wail of a saxophone and pounding of drums reached Anna's ears. Her toes tapped as the musicians poured out their tune.

"Wait until we get inside. This will be a good night." Dottie linked arms with Anna and pulled her through the door. "Can't you feel it?"

Anna sashayed into the large hall. Spring flowers decorated the windows and tables that lined the walls. A piano stood crammed in a corner, surrounded by a hodgepodge of musicians. She inhaled the scent of flowers mixed with the press of bodies. Her shoulders relaxed, and she could feel it. Dottie was right. Tonight would be a good night.

Her gaze landed on Specialist Chance. A lazy grin creased his face as he nodded her way. Was he pulling his dance partner closer? Anna gasped as he winked at her over the shoulder of the girl he spun around the floor. She turned her back and flounced to the refreshments table. She could hear Dottie's heels clack against the floor as she followed.

The music ended, and she stiffened. He wouldn't dare approach her after that display! Someone tapped her shoulder. She resisted turning, but curiosity got the better of her.

"Dance with me?" Sid stood there, the same easy grin on his face.

The insufferable man saw nothing wrong with what he'd done. Anna stiffened and thrust a cup of punch at him. "Hold this. It's the closest you'll get to holding me."

She spun and walked toward the entrance. Where had Dottie disappeared? Anna had to get away from him and the laughter that followed her.

Why did he have to be so insufferable and easy on the eyes at the same time?

seven

May 25, 1944

Anna shimmered in the light, her blue dress skimming her figure as she hurried away. Sid couldn't take his eyes off her. She wouldn't get away from him that easily. He followed her to a corner, where she grabbed the arm of a gal who looked vaguely familiar, but then, most of the gals here did. "Let's start again. Good evening, Miss Goodman."

She startled as she spun and met his gaze. "Specialist Chance. You don't give up, do you?"

"Not when it involves a beautiful woman."

The gal with her looked between the two of them then unhooked arms with Anna. "Looks like your first dance arrived. Told you it'd be fun." With a wave of her fingers, she headed toward the punch table, leaving the two of them alone. Anna stared after her, her stance stiffening subtly.

The first notes of "Boogie Woogie Bugle Boy" filled the air, and Sid bopped his head to the beat. He cleared his throat and reached for her hand. "Join me?"

"What? The other girl won't dance anymore?"

"I'm not asking her."

"Maybe you should." She blew out a breath. "I am not another girl to add to a long list of conquests. If that's what you're looking for, then kindly walk away." Sparks lit her eyes. She had no idea how enchanting her anger made her.

"No. You're the girl I want to dance with this evening." He offered his hand again, and her chin tipped as if to challenge him even as her hand slid into his.

"You really don't want to dance with me."

"I can't imagine why not."

39

"I've danced with Clark Gable. He sets a high standard."

"That's funny. I've heard he has two left feet."

"Merely a rumor from *Gone with the Wind*." A smile softened her lips with a hint of promise that left him wondering.

He led her to the floor, and they started a quick jitterbug. By the time the song ended, color tinged her cheeks. The stress and worries that burdened her when he saw her on the farm evaporated before his eyes. Something about her captured him. Made him want to learn more. The band slid into a beat that had some swing to it, and she followed his lead as if they'd practiced many times. It felt like they were in a Fred Astaire and Ginger Rogers movie as they glided around the floor with the other couples.

He lost track of time as song melted into song. After three or four, he pulled her to the side. "How about some punch?"

"Sounds wonderful." She fanned her face. "I'm a bit out of practice."

"So how did I do?" He led her to the table and offered her a cup of the red liquid.

"What?" Mischief filled her eyes. "Well, I didn't jitterbug with Mr. Gable, so I can't compare. I'd say you held your own, soldier."

Sid wiped imaginary sweat off his brow. Anna took a drink then placed her empty cup on a tray. Before she could say anything, a soldier approached her.

"May I have a dance, ma'am?"

Anna glanced at Sid, and he shrugged. Much as he'd like to keep her to himself, he didn't have the right, any more than she should have been angry when she saw him with someone else. Even so, as she walked away on the other man's arm, his chest tightened. Maybe he'd need to change their status.

❧

The next week dragged as Sid wondered when he could see Anna again. The image of her from the USO filled his thoughts. She'd been so full of life. He wanted to learn how to bring the butterfly out of her self-imposed cocoon. Too often, she lived like she'd forgotten how to enjoy life.

He walked the perimeter of the Shivelys' sugar beet field. The denim shirts of a dozen PWs dotted the field, easy to spot among the low crop. Sid stifled a yawn. The morning had begun earlier than usual in order to get the men to the farm with plenty of time to work.

Word had spread. The demand for labor had him driving all over southern Nebraska.

At noon, the farmer's wife and children lugged out baskets filled with sandwiches and well water for the men. They dug in heartily while Sid and Trent counted noses.

Sid stopped and counted again. "Tell me I've missed someone. We're short one."

"Impossible. Where would he go?"

"Get the list out of the truck. We should have a dozen men."

Trent hustled to the truck and returned with the clipboard. "I double-checked. Twelve prisoners are on the roll."

Sid shoved his hands deep in his pockets as he struggled to explain how they had eleven. He couldn't imagine the flack if they lost a prisoner or one escaped.

"I count eleven, too." Trent tossed the clipboard at Sid, his face white as a sheet.

The two spent the next hour scouring the farm and interviewing the prisoners without success.

Sid hung his head in his hands. "How does a prisoner disappear?"

"Do you want me to rouse the alarm at Camp Atlanta?" Trent looked at him as though the answer had better be no.

"No. I'll handle that and take the other prisoners back. I don't believe they didn't see anything."

Trent shrugged. "Maybe their jobs absorbed them."

"No, they're covering for their buddy." Sid scanned the horizon again. Nothing but fields surrounded them, with an occasional farmhouse visible on the horizon. "Round them up."

The drive to camp passed too quickly. In no time, he'd returned the prisoners to Compound A and stood in front of the camp commander, trying to explain.

Commander Moss sat behind his desk, a dark scowl on his face. The man prided himself in running a tight ship. "Where's Private Franklin?"

"Searching the farm, sir." Sid stood at attention, back stiff, as he waited for the verdict. Kitchen patrol couldn't be too terrible, right? His mom had made sure he knew how to use a potato peeler. He'd survive KP.

Commander Moss ran his hands over his thinning hair, his eyes fixed in the distance as if developing a course of action. "You were at Fort Robinson with the war dogs, right?"

"Yes, sir."

"All right. Take five men and the bloodhounds. Sniff out the prisoner."

Sid swallowed and considered the task. He'd worked with many dogs but never with bloodhounds. "Are they trained search dogs?"

"Consider this a training exercise. One that can't fail."

"Yes, sir."

"I'll notify the sheriff and town police. We have to find this man before he gets away."

Sid saluted then collected five men from the barracks. A vague uneasiness filled him at the thought of using bloodhounds. He'd prefer any dog he'd trained at Fort Robinson instead.

None of the men he'd found had experience with war dogs, though a couple hunted. He hoped those skills would transfer to a search like this. "Any of you work with dogs when you hunted?"

A couple of blank stares met his. Then one soldier nodded. "We had a mongrel that went with us. She was pretty handy at bringing back the fowl. She never treed a man, though, if that's what you mean."

"I'll take any experience. We'll pick up a few bloodhounds then head to the farm. Private Franklin and I noticed this prisoner missing at lunchtime." Sid glanced at his watch.

"It's now four. The other prisoners claim they didn't see him slip away. Since we can't pinpoint a time, he could have quite a head start on us. We'll start on the farm, see what the hounds pick up. We'll fan out from there."

"And when we find him?"

"We bring him back. In one piece. We don't know he tried to escape."

"Sure. He wandered off."

"Maybe. Our job is to find him, not try him. Let's head out."

The men climbed into the bed of the truck, and after picking up the hounds at the barn, Sid returned to the Shively farm, which stood within a mile of the Goodman place.

Mr. Shively met the truck at the barn. His overalls strained to contain his stomach as he marched toward them. "It's about time you got back. Private Franklin's scouring the hills while you're off gallivanting."

Sid took a deep breath and tamped down the flare of heat filling him. "Where is Private Franklin?"

"Off that way." Mr. Shively waved in a northerly direction. "You'd better find that man before something happens. Maybe he's headed to Kearney to sabotage the air base."

"Then he'll walk a long way." Sid turned and found himself face-to-face with seven other men. Some looked familiar. Must have prisoners on their farms periodically. "We'll find him."

The men stared at him with hard eyes, broad shoulders set in firm lines. One clutched a shotgun. Sid looked from man to man, taking each one's measure. This situation could turn ugly in an instant, and he didn't want the fallout. He had to find the prisoner before the locals turned vigilante. He hurried back to the soldiers waiting by the truck.

"We'll break into groups of two, each with a dog, and head into the field the prisoners worked today." He watched the bloodhounds mill around. He didn't have any way to alert the dogs to the scent they should track. Without that, he doubted they'd help at all. "Let's move. Private Franklin is somewhere in front of us. Keep your eyes peeled."

Hours later, as the sun sank low on the horizon, Sid wiped sweat from under his cap brim. His feet were sore, his skin itched, and he hadn't the first clue which direction the prisoner had gone. The only good news was that they'd found Trent.

"Any ideas?"

Trent gulped a swig of water from his canteen. "We covered this farm. Unless we move to the next ones, we're done. Problem is which direction to explore. There's nothing to track."

"I'll head back to the farmhouse and call the command post. Maybe somebody had better luck."

Trent snorted. "This land's too wide open. There's nothing to stop him from walking to Kansas or hopping a train."

"But where would he run? His clothes are clearly labeled. He has no papers to get out of the country. And he barely speaks ten words of English."

After checking with the camp, Sid determined that none of the search parties had found the prisoner yet. He also hadn't shown up in his barracks.

Sid returned to the group of men waiting on the ground around the truck. "Nobody's had any luck. We're to check the nearby farms. Trent and I will take his Jeep." He tossed the truck keys to another soldier. "You can drive the rest of the men back to Atlanta. Take the east road, and check the farms on the way back. Don't forget the barns and outbuildings."

After stopping at another farm, Trent pulled into the Goodmans' driveway. "You get to talk to Goodman."

Sid nodded and jogged to the door. Knock, ask his questions, and leave. It wouldn't take long, and they'd be off. Though if Anna had come home, he'd love an excuse to stay. One look inside the kitchen, and he forgot about Anna. The prisoner sat, back straight, in a tall kitchen chair, Mr. Goodman leaning over him with a gun.

"Look what the wind blew in." Mr. Goodman limped

toward Sid. "I was about ready to walk him to Camp Atlanta for you boys."

"I'll escort him to camp, sir." Sid approached the prisoner. He appeared unharmed, though an unusual glow filled his eyes. Sid eased between the two men, a knot forming in his belly at the thought that this prisoner might be a rare, hard-core Nazi. He'd return the man and let the commander sort out the prisoner's status.

Mr. Goodman pulled his gun to his chest, then nodded. "Get him off my property. He's the kind I fought in the last war. I don't like him on my farm."

"Come with me." Sid grabbed the prisoner's arm and tugged him to his feet. "Thanks for your help."

Mr. Goodman sank into his chair and grabbed a bottle. He took a swig from it, clearly ignoring them. Maybe lost in a sea of memories from the earlier war.

Sid backed the prisoner out the door and into the Jeep. Trent sat next to him, hand on his gun, as they raced back to Camp Atlanta. Sid whispered a prayer that God would free Mr. Goodman and his family of the effects of the last war.

eight

Round, multicolored balls hung from the tree, and the scent of fresh-cut pine mixed with apple cider. Mama snuggled next to Papa on the couch, her hand tucked firmly in his. A soft expression crossed his face as he gazed at her. Anna watched from the chair beside the fireplace. Brent rolled on the ground with Patches, the Australian shepherd that roamed the fields with the guys during the day and curled up in the kitchen at night. Strains of Bing Crosby crooning "White Christmas" crackled from the old phonograph.

Anna relaxed into the dream, reluctant to release the memories. Had only two years passed since love overflowed in her life?

"Good morning, sleepyhead."

Anna groaned as something or someone bounced onto her bed. She squinted up at Dottie. "Can't you let a girl sleep?"

"Not when we have to get to work. Come on. You'll miss the bus if you don't hurry."

"But I have a secret weapon."

"Oh?" Dottie cocked an eyebrow at her, tapping her fingers on her arms. "What could that be, pray tell?"

"Your car."

"Good ol' Stube." Dottie frowned even as she mentioned her beloved Studebaker. "He's low on gas, so if we want to get home tomorrow, we'll have to bus it."

Anna rolled out of bed and reached for the coveralls waiting on the bedside chair. "These don't get any more glamorous."

"Nope. Each day they look the same."

"Good thing I'm not planning on turning any guy's head."

"Definitely won't if you don't hustle."

Anna tuned out Dottie's babble as she rushed to get ready

for the factory. After running to catch the bus, Anna puffed out a breath of air. The morning held the promise of a hot day that could turn stifling in the parachute packing area. Crates loaded with supplies for the jungle packs lined the room when they arrived.

Grabbing a canvas pack, she joined the line of women. First, she stuffed in a pair of leather gloves, then a large knife, compass, and fishhooks in a container. She stepped to the next series of boxes and prayed that if a soldier ever used the pack, God would keep him safe. Field rations, mosquito lotion, matches, and a red fuse joined the other items. After adding several packets of medicine, Anna sealed the kit and added it to the growing stash. The supplies ran out before her prayers did.

The work didn't tax her, yet by the end of the day, she felt ready to crawl into bed and pull the covers over her head. Despite her prayers, the papers were filled with casualty lists.

Rumors flew that the big push to reenter the European continent would come this summer. She hated to imagine the loss of life bound to accompany such an assault. And Brent's crew lived and flew somewhere near the coming combat. He tried to keep his letters light, but Anna sensed things he couldn't write. Her heart clenched at the danger each time his B-17 joined a bombing run. Too few crews experienced the success of the *Memphis Belle*. That B-17 crew's angels had worked overtime to bring them home after twenty-five missions.

If only Brent lived under the same protection. Anna wanted to hope. But reality forced her to be honest with herself. It would take a miracle.

No wonder her mind sought happier times during her dreams.

❧

Saturday morning, Anna walked the periphery of the farmyard between chores. The place looked worse than only a week earlier. Signs of neglect abounded, from the peeling paint on the house to the loose boards in the fence around Nellie's pen. Good thing the cow was too old to run far even if she wanted to.

God, I need some help here. Some fresh ideas to get Papa moving again.

As she walked, several options ran through her mind. Maybe she should quit her job at the air base. But what would they do without the cash? Maybe she could find someone to live at the farm during the week. She thought of her purse balance and knew she couldn't pay anyone enough to put up with Papa.

The weight pressed into her until she feared she'd topple forward into the dirt. She didn't have the strength to pretend Papa was okay. But she also didn't know how to change anything. Reality wouldn't change because she wished it.

Gravel spun under tires. Anna didn't recognize the pickup truck headed down the drive. It looked government issue. Her stomach churned at the thought that Specialist Chance may have brought a load of prisoners with him. She couldn't imagine who else would stop by the farm. Papa had pushed away all of their friends since Mama's death. She ran her hands across her pants then pushed her hair behind her ears. She'd enjoy sparring with him, but Papa's mood wouldn't allow prisoners to swarm the fields.

She held her breath and shielded her eyes as she waited to see if anyone joined him.

Sid opened the door of the truck but didn't wait for anyone. "Morning."

Anna stepped back at the distance in his tone. He wasn't here to see her, and she tensed, waiting for him to explain his presence.

"I. . ." Sid cleared his throat and shoved his hands in his pant pockets. "Anna, we need to talk about your father."

She hugged her arms around her middle. "What do you mean?"

"He didn't tell you about what happened a couple days ago?"

"You'd better explain what you mean."

"A prisoner wandered away from the Shively place. We tracked him here." Sid widened his stance, as if to brace against her reaction. "Your father had him cornered in the kitchen. A gun pointed at him."

Throbbing filled her temples. She tried to rub the pain away, but the pounding only intensified. "I'll take care of it."

"How? You aren't here during the week."

"Sorry, I can't be here and do my part for the war effort. Maybe you should focus on keeping track of your prisoners. Seems that's the easy solution."

The silence stretched as red crept up his neck. Maybe Sid hadn't done anything to lose the prisoner, but she didn't care.

"I have work. As you pointed out, I'm only here on weekends." She hurried into the barn before he could see the tears pooling in the corners of her eyes. She waited until she heard the slam of the truck door before venturing toward Nellie. Even then, her hands trembled. She'd find a way to do something about Papa. She had to before he did something crazier than trapping a prisoner in their house.

❧

Sid slapped his cap on the seat next to him. That woman could raise his blood pressure faster than anyone else he'd ever met. What gave her the right to walk away without finishing the conversation? Then again, what gave him the right to barge onto her farm to tell her everything she did wrong?

It wasn't her fault her father acted crazy. Nor did she have anything to do with the prisoner escapade.

He pointed the truck back toward Camp Atlanta. Much as he might wish to be anywhere else right now, his duty lay there. The ribbing from the guys hadn't stopped since he and Trent had brought the prisoner back. Crazy thing was, he still didn't know how the guy slipped away. Post intelligence had spent time with him, but answers weren't any clearer now than they'd been on Wednesday.

The system had built-in slack. Only so many soldiers stationed at Camp Atlanta could serve as guards. Most farmers checked out their prisoners as needed with no supervision at all. His luck hadn't held. That was all. It had to happen at some point. With almost three thousand prisoners, sooner or later one would disappear or try to escape. The next would learn from this attempt. The Goodman farm required a wide berth if you wanted a change of scenery.

Maybe he'd get lucky and get moved to one of the satellite camps springing up across the state. Then he might escape the reputation as the only soldier to lose a prisoner.

He glanced at his watch and pressed down on the accelerator. Commander Moss wouldn't appreciate his arriving late to the policy and procedures meeting—an emergency meeting in response to the fiasco.

He pulled into a spot in front of the administration building and hopped out. The building mirrored the others on base. The Army Corps of Engineers had spread a concrete foundation roughly 25 by 150 feet and thrown up tar-sheeting walls and a roof.

The camp wasn't designed to last more than a few years, just till the war ended. A far cry from the permanence of the brick buildings and barns that lined the parade grounds at Fort Robinson.

Sid opened the door and took a chair toward the back of the lecture room.

"Nice of you to join us, Specialist Chance." Commander Moss frowned at Sid. "Approach the front and update everyone on Wednesday's events."

Sid hesitated as he tried to collect his thoughts. He stood and briefed the assembled officers. "Any questions?" He sank into his chair when there were none.

"Here's how procedures will change. We haven't had trouble to date, and frankly, we've been lucky. I've already assigned men to work more closely with each camp liaison as we screen prisoners to detect troublemakers. We'll also watch for homesick blokes." Moss paced the front of the room.

"Our job is to get these men safely through the duration

so we can send them home to their country and families."
He paused and pierced Sid with his stare. "We can't end the
prisoner program on farms. Their labor is too valuable, and
it keeps them occupied in productive endeavors. We'll have
no more than ten men to every two guards. As soon as the
prisoners become proficient, we'll lower the number at each
farm.

"The key: Remain vigilant. We don't want this to happen
again. Let's work with the community to keep the prisoners
content. Hopefully we won't face many more situations."

Sounded great to Sid, but how would it really work? There
were too many prisoners to monitor. Too many needs to
meet.

nine

June 4, 1944

The smell of bacon sizzling on the stove filled the kitchen. Anna hoped it would pull Papa out of bed. She'd leave for church in an hour, and he needed to make the trip with her.

Her mind and heart continued to seesaw between disappointment and hope. Yesterday's announcement that the invasion of France had started had sent her hopes and fears skyrocketing as she whispered prayers for all the boys in uniform. Then the news that the attack hadn't started flooded her with relief, followed by anxiety that the battle would come soon.

How could she focus on Papa when so many other crises erupted all over the world?

Nobody else would take care of Papa, and he certainly didn't care. All week she'd prayed about what to do. All she could think was that he needed to get out of the house. Focus on something or someone other than the grief he clung to. And what better place to start than with a worship service? He hadn't attended one since Mama's funeral. High time he attended to important matters and relationships.

Anna tucked an errant strand of hair behind her ear. Getting him out of bed before noon would be challenge enough. She'd let the bacon talk for her.

Twenty minutes later, the eggs and bacon had cooled, the toast toughened.

"I won't give up that easily." Anna marched toward his bedroom door. She squared her shoulders and knocked. "Papa, time to get up. Breakfast is cold."

A noise like a grunt served as his response.

"Now, Papa. You know you like a hot breakfast. Come on. It's after nine, and I finished the chores hours ago."

"Go away."

"Not until you talk to me." Anna stamped her foot. Why was he so insufferable?

Curses echoed against the door as he stomped around his room. He threw open the door, and Anna jumped back. A dark cloud covered his features. "What do you want?" With each word, his voice rose until he yelled the last.

Anna tipped her chin up and stared. "If you'd care to put your robe on, breakfast is served. It might even be warm."

"I ain't hungry."

"Well." Anna floundered for words. Where had her conviction fled? Somewhere into the anger boiling in his eyes. It didn't matter. He had to change, and she'd do whatever she could to force the subject. "Papa, I'd like you to go to church with me."

He sputtered. "What gave you a crazy idea like that, girl? I vowed at your Mama's funeral that I would never darken the door of a church again. God didn't care for her, and she was a good woman."

"That's not true. He loves us all. Papa, something is eating away at you. It'll destroy you if we don't do something. I can't stand to watch that happen any longer. Please."

A flicker of pain flashed across his face. He shouldered past her as if pushing past the memories and emotions. "I think I'll eat some of that breakfast now."

Anna sagged against the doorframe. She wouldn't give up. He meant too much to her. He flopped into a chair at the table then shoveled food on his plate. By the mound heaped there, he'd be eating long after she left.

"I'll be back after service."

Papa didn't bother to answer as she grabbed her hat and purse and headed out the door.

The old Ford practically laughed at her when she tried to start it. After several false starts, it roared to life. She glanced at the gas gauge and hoped enough remained to get her to town. The white clapboard Cornerstone Community Church, nestled in the heart of Holdrage, finally came into view.

Gus Powell and Teddy Whitaker stood by the front door, opening it for the families approaching the building. Salt and pepper colored their hair, and their shoulders sloped, evidence of the long days each had worked. The two used to sit by the fire at her house for hours in the winter, playing checkers and chess with Papa. Maybe they'd come today.

Anna's steps quickened at the thought. Help might be that simple to arrange. They'd known her dad since grade school. The long tales they liked to weave might help him forget and pull him back into the thick of life.

"Well, hello, Miss Anna." Gus wolf-whistled. "Don't you look smart."

Anna held out her navy polka-dot skirt and twirled. Her hand touched her chin as she curtsied to the two.

"Lovely as a picture." Teddy offered his arm, which she accepted. "Let me escort you in to the service."

"I'd love that. I have a question first."

"Shoot."

"Could you two join Papa and me for dinner after church?"

"I don't see your Daddy anywhere." Gus frowned as he pretended to search the sidewalk.

"I know." Anna shrugged. "I don't know what to do anymore. I thought your visit might pull him out of his mood."

The large bell atop the church rang. Anna jumped at the loud sound that boomed from directly overhead. Teddy patted her arm.

"Let's get you inside. I'll bring this lug with me to dinner."

Tears pricked her eyes at the thought of what their presence could mean. "Thank you."

"Don't worry." Teddy's eyes clouded over, maybe with thoughts of his own dear wife in heaven. "Your daddy'll pull out of this funk he's in. It takes us all different amounts of time and prayer to move on. Besides, we'll help push him out if he's stuck."

Gus chuckled. "Pushing him'll be like convincing a pheasant to go where you want. Sounds like a good challenge to me."

Teddy escorted Anna through the doors and toward a seat near the back. She settled in between Mrs. Manahan and the end of the pew, then shifted as she tried to find a comfortable spot next to Mrs. Manahan's wide girth. The frown the woman shot Anna stilled her efforts. Mrs. Manahan had been her mother's best friend, but she frowned on disruptions of any kind, especially those that didn't fit in the life-or-death category.

While Pastor Reynolds intoned the announcements, Anna tried to create a menu for lunch. Gus and Teddy were simple men, widowers who'd walked the road Papa now traveled. Anna hoped they could reach him where she'd failed. The organ burst into life, and Anna stood with the rest of the congregation. The men would be happy to eat anything they hadn't cooked. If only the cupboard weren't so bare. She shook herself. She'd think of something. This meal would be worth every bit of effort.

The service passed in a blur as Anna's thoughts ping-ponged between prayers for Papa and Brent and flurries of fear that Papa would reject his friends. She hated that possibility, but what else could she do?

She lingered toward the back of the church while she waited for Teddy and Gus after the service. Gus seemed intent on greeting every person who'd attended—again— while Teddy straightened the abandoned pews. Anna tried not to rock, even though she knew how antsy her daddy would be getting.

Finally, Anna glanced at her watch and headed toward Gus. She waited, hands clutching her purse while he greeted Mr. and Mrs. Conway. "I'm heading to the farm unless you and Teddy need a ride."

"Oh no. We'll be fine." He turned his broad smile on another family. "See you next week."

What would the pastor do without Gus to greet everyone? Anna smiled in spite of the vise that gripped her stomach. "All right. Come as soon as you can."

Gus scanned the emptying sanctuary. "Shouldn't be much longer." He whistled sharply, causing Anna to jump. "Right, Teddy?"

"What?" The man stopped collecting Bibles and frowned at Gus.

"We'll be at the Goodman place soon."

"Sure. Sure." Teddy shook his head and muttered as he returned to work.

Anna slipped out before anyone could stop her. As soon as she reached the house, Papa started grumbling.

"Where have you been? I'm downright starved."

"At church. I'll have dinner ready soon."

"Church? This long? This is exactly why it's a waste of time to attend."

Anna's heart clenched at his harsh words. She grabbed one of Mama's aprons. "Could you grab some potatoes from the cellar?"

Muttering under his breath, he shuffled from the room in the general direction of the cellar. Anna rubbed her forehead, trying to ease the pain that pounded whenever he came near, and set to work slicing ham. By the time Gus and Teddy pulled into the yard, the room smelled like ham, potatoes, and biscuits.

"Papa, you've got company."

"What on earth?"

"Come and see."

Gus and Teddy stood on the step, their faces wreathed with grins. Papa opened the door and stared. Gus stuck out his hand. "Where're you keeping yourself, stranger? We've missed you at the café."

Papa seemed to relax as the men chatted about nothing

in the living room. Anna leaned against the sink and soaked in the sound of his laughter. It had been so long since she'd heard the once-familiar sound.

She called them to the table and served the simple meal. Then she slipped away, tears streaming down her cheeks, and stood around the corner listening.

Maybe God had heard her prayer for help.

Three hours later when Dottie finally picked her up, Anna wasn't so sure. Papa shut down the moment Gus and Teddy left. Then he turned on her, rage mottling his face.

"I don't like you interfering, girl." He stormed around the kitchen then flipped on the radio with a force that had it rocking on the counter. "Leave Gus and Teddy out of this."

She'd backed into a wall in an attempt to stay out of his reach. If Dottie hadn't arrived, she didn't want to think what Papa would have done. She'd never seen him like this. And after he'd been friendly with his buddies. She didn't understand the mood swings.

All she knew was she didn't think she could come home again. But if she didn't, who would ensure there was a farm left when this war ended and Brent finally came home?

As Dottie's Stube rattled down the road away from the farm, Anna realized Sid hadn't appeared all weekend. Had Papa scared him away, too?

ten

June 5, 1944

A knock rattled the door to Anna's bedroom at the Wisdoms'. She cracked her eyes but couldn't see anything. She groaned and rolled over. Why would anyone pound on their door in the middle of the night?

Dottie elbowed Anna when the door shook again. "Go see what's up."

Anna stifled a yawn. "Why me? You're the night owl. You get it."

"Oh no. It can't be good news." Dottie's voice sounded strangled.

Reaching for her robe, Anna slid out of bed. "Who is it?"

"Mr. Wisdom. I think you'll want to come downstairs, ladies. There's news on the radio."

Anna tied her belt and hurried to open the door. She cracked it. "Thank you. We'll be right there." After FDR's earlier fireside chat about the fall of Rome, what could be so important?

Hot cups of peppermint tea sat on the kitchen table when Anna and Dottie hurried into the room. Anna wrapped her arms around her stomach, desperate to still the tremor that threatened to shake her to pieces. The Wisdoms and other boarders sat huddled around the kitchen table and the radio.

"Someone tell me what's happening." Dottie's voice cracked on the words.

Mr. Wisdom motioned her to a chair. "Eisenhower launched the invasion of France."

Anna relaxed. "Probably another false alarm. You know how the rumors have flown."

"No, the reports sound real, but we're only hearing random details." Jessica Ferguson huddled in a chair. Anna wondered if her thoughts focused on her fiancé, who'd shipped to Britain months ago. Part of the infantry, he'd surely participate in the real invasion.

Anna glanced at the wall clock. Almost ten thirty. She wished an announcement, any announcement, would come. Was the invasion real? How was it going? Were the casualties high?

The murmur of voices soon overshadowed the radio broadcast.

"Shh." Mrs. Wisdom smiled as she waved everyone down. "I know we're all anxious, but no one can hear if we're all talking."

Uncomfortable silence settled on the room. The strains of an orchestra flowed from NBC. While it sounded nice, it wasn't what Anna wanted to hear:

❧

"In a few seconds, we will take you to London for the first eyewitness account of the actual invasion of France by sea— of the landing of Allied troops on a French beachhead. War correspondent George Hicks saw those landings from the bridge of an Allied warship, and through the ingenuity of radio wire recording, the National Broadcasting Company is able to give you the story as witnessed by George Hicks in a pool broadcast. So, now, NBC takes you to London for the first eyewitness account of the actual invasion of Europe!"

❧

Anna held her breath as nothing but static came across. The seconds ticked by while Dottie chewed on a fingernail. The subdued voice of George Hicks filled the room. Anna released a breath she hadn't realized she'd held. The noise of planes passing overhead served as a backdrop to his narrative. In midsentence, static again interrupted, and everyone groaned.

The group stayed glued to the radio into the early morning hours, no one able to tear away from the sporadic updates.

Yet the musical interludes drove Anna crazy. It didn't seem right to have swing music playing while the infantry attacked the beaches of France.

"It's really started." Anna's heart constricted. Where was Brent? Did he man one of the bombers paving the way for the infantry? She tried to pray for him and all the other boys she knew fighting somewhere around the world, but the words choked off in her mind.

God, help them. Help them all.

The next morning dawned much too early. Anna buried her head under the pillow, wishing for the oblivion of dreams. There war didn't exist. Mama still lived. Life felt normal. Reality intruded with the sun's rays.

"Do you think anyone will work today?" Dottie's sleepy voice tugged Anna awake.

"Until we know, we have to treat it like every other day."

Dottie propped herself up on her elbows. "Are you kidding? We're finally doing something offensive in Europe. That doesn't make today like yesterday or last week."

The image of American boys scrambling to reclaim French soil from the German army flooded her mind. Anna tried to block out the accompanying sight of bombs exploding and bullets flying. "What else do you want to do? Curl up here and pretend nothing happened? Or get back to work and do something that will help all those soldiers? Maybe today some of the men are wearing the parachutes we packed." She sighed and wiped her hands across her face. "We have to go to work until they tell us to go home. There's too much left to do."

"I hate this feeling." Dottie threw back her covers. "It's like I'm sitting on pins and needles, waiting to see if the assault worked."

"We won't learn anything staying in bed."

When the bus reached the air base, the air vibrated with sound for once not caused by the rumbling B-17s flying overhead. Instead, nervous energy seemed to consume everyone, as if they couldn't decide whether to work harder than ever for the boys invading the beaches of France or to run to the nearest church and pray.

&

Sid examined his group of men. In the aftermath of the beginning of the Normandy invasion, Commander Moss had each group running through their paces. They'd be well-oiled units either to avoid a repeat of a prisoner disappearing or to join the battle overseas. Each time he thought about the prisoner fiasco, Sid wanted to head straight to the nearest battle. France would suit him just fine.

"Ten-hut. To the lecture hall." Commander Moss wanted the rank and file to hear more about the escape, disappearance, loss, whatever you wanted to call it. Sid called it embarrassing.

An hour later, Sid was more than ready to get away from Camp Atlanta for a while. He accepted the assignment to deliver a load of prisoners to the Kearney air base with a grin. Trent joined him for backup, and they rounded up the skilled carpenters from among the prisoners.

The wind whistled through the truck cab as miles rolled along. The drive took a little over an hour; then Sid presented the paperwork at the guard station.

"Do you know where you're headed?" The baby-faced soldier hardly looked old enough to carry a gun, and he served as the first line of defense? Guess sabotage wasn't a big concern.

Sid glanced at the papers. "Nope. Want to point us in the right direction?"

"Head down this road and turn left at your first chance. Follow that road till you see the signs."

"Thanks." Sid put the truck in gear. "Guess we'll be there in no time."

Trent eased lower in the seat and leaned against the backrest. "So what do we do while the prisoners work?"

"Keep an eye on them."

"And any pretty girls we spot?" Trent let out a wolf whistle.

"Those girls look like they could use some new friends."

"Focus. We've got a job to do."

"Babysit a few prisoners who'd stand out like a sore thumb if they tried anything? Give me a real job." A sour frown sagged Trent's face. "Days like today, I want to join the fight overseas."

"You and me both. But Uncle Sam in his wisdom has us stationed here. So let's focus on the assignment. Our day could still come, but only if we do what's needed now. Besides, someone has to take care of all the prisoners."

"Not what I signed up for."

"Maybe, but you've got to follow orders."

"Can't blame a guy for wishing."

Sid thought about the guys trying to gain a foothold on the beaches of France. When would they know more information? The world was too big at times like this. The snatches of radio broadcasts he'd heard only let him know the fight was real.

"Hey, isn't that the girl from the Goodman farm?" Trent poked Sid in the ribs. Sid swerved to keep the truck on the road.

"Watch it." Once he knew the truck wouldn't roll, he turned the direction Trent pointed. "Looks like it. Let's get these prisoners dropped off."

"Then you can track her down and take her to lunch. You'd have better luck if you stopped and asked her now while you know where she is."

Sid watched her walk in the direction the truck had come from. For once, Trent had a good idea. Finding her later could be impossible since he didn't know which building she worked in. And the idea of asking around for her did not appeal to him. He eased the truck into an open space on the side of the street. "Watch the boys."

"Yes, sir." Trent winked as he saluted. "Good luck, sir."

Sid slapped him with his cap before pushing it back on his head and hopping out of the truck. He glanced down the street and saw her about a block behind him. He hustled after her. "Anna."

The woman stopped then eased toward him. A frown creased her face before the light of recognition dawned. "What are you doing here, Sid?"

"Wondering if you'd like to have lunch with me in a bit." He stood at ease while he waited. The seconds ticked by as she considered him.

"I still don't understand why you're here."

"Delivering some prisoners. Thought if you had time, we could grab a bite."

A smile started in her eyes and spread to her lips. "I'd like that."

"Where can I meet you?"

"The mess hall is fine. I need to finish this errand. Can you meet me there in thirty minutes?"

Sid had no idea where the mess hall stood, but he could find it if it meant spending time with the woman in front of him.

As if reading his mind, she stepped back. "See you then."

A honk interrupted his thoughts as he watched her walk away. After another glance at her, he hurried back to the truck. Time to get the prisoners delivered.

After a few wrong turns, Sid pulled the truck in front of the building housing the post engineer. He and Trent turned the prisoners over to the corporal on duty and were told not to come back until 1700 hours.

They returned to the truck, and Trent leaned against it. "Guess you have plans for lunch."

"Want to join us?"

"And be the third wheel? No thanks. I'll find someone else to entertain with my charm. Meet you here at 1700." Trent walked away, whistling, his hands stuffed in his pockets.

Sid left the truck and headed in the general direction of the mess hall. He asked for directions a couple of times before finally locating the correct building. Like so many buildings on base, the engineers had built it quickly, and it already showed signs of wear from the harsh Nebraska weather. He didn't care what the building looked like as long as the food was decent and he shared it with Anna.

She stood inside the door, foot tapping.

"Have you waited long?" He swiped his hat off and shoved it in his back pocket.

"No." Circles he hadn't noticed earlier shadowed her eyes. Even with her canvas work coveralls and obvious fatigue, she carried herself like royalty.

He offered her his arm. "Let's feed you before you have to get back to work."

"I don't know that there's a rush today."

He quirked an eyebrow at her.

"Everyone seems distracted by the news, or lack of it, about the invasion. Have you heard anything?"

"Only what's on the radio."

"You'd think we'd have access to better information working at military installations." She shrugged.

They traveled the cafeteria line, loading their trays with food, and then he led the way to a table. Time passed quickly as he told her stories of growing up in St. Louis. Their backgrounds were vastly different. Big city versus small-town farm. Large family versus small. Yet as he watched her laugh at a story, he knew they could build a solid friendship. And if he could keep her laughing, maybe it could turn into something much more.

eleven

Luka and Otto worked alongside several other prisoners in one of the Goodman fields. The prisoners were getting the rhythm of pulling the weeds that grew between the wavy rows of corn. They'd come a long way since their first visit to the farm. Even so, it'd take several days to eradicate all the weeds that had sprung up since the last round of rain.

The sun beat down on Sid's head. He looked for shade but couldn't spot even a shrub to provide some relief. The prisoners had to feel the heat, too. The corn wasn't tall enough to provide even sporadic shade.

He glanced at the house. At many other farms, the prisoners would be invited in for lunch, despite regulations. In turn, he'd disappear for a bit so the prisoners could interact with the families. The prisoners had an intense curiosity about the American way of life. So much of what they'd learned in Germany didn't match the farms' reality. The exposure could only help in the postwar days.

"Specialist Chance?"

Sid turned to Luka. "Yes?"

Luka looked pale under his white cap. "May we break for water?"

"Grab your canteens from the truck."

Luka whistled, and the other prisoners gathered around him. As the weeks passed, Luka had stepped into a leadership role. He translated Sid's instructions accurately, making it easier on the prisoners and the guards. In a few more weeks, Sid thought he could trust Luka to keep a small group of prisoners in line without a guard. Even with the escape attempt, the commander had decided the requests for labor plus the sheer number of prisoners compared to the smaller group of soldiers stationed at Camp Atlanta and the satellite prisons made it critical to get as many prisoners as possible ready to work on their own. The administration clerks worked hard to match trusted prisoners with cooperative farmers.

Mr. Goodman wouldn't make that list anytime soon.

❧

Friday night, an army truck sat next to the barn when Dottie pulled her car into the Goodman yard. Anna looked from the house to the truck. Hadn't Sid heard any of her arguments for why they couldn't afford extra labor? Or had he come to see her? Heat climbed her neck at the thought. Since their lunch, she'd looked forward to seeing him again.

She eyed the house, dread gripping her. If Papa remained in the same foul mood she'd left him in, she couldn't stay.

"Are you getting out or coming home with me?" The concern in Dottie's eyes softened the edge to her words.

"I'm sorry." Anna grabbed her bag and turned to Dottie. "I just hope Papa's ready for some company."

"You can always call, and I'll come get you." Dottie pulled her close for a hug. "It'll be okay, and you're only here until we can find some soldier to sweep you off your feet."

If only it were that simple. Dottie deliberately forgot that the farm didn't have a phone—or electricity for that matter. The lines hadn't made it that far. And she refused to understand the depth of responsibility Anna carried. Maybe her multiple siblings at home made it easier for Dottie to slide in and out of home life. She could work in Kearney and come home for fun. Anna came home to hold everything together for another week.

"Don't look now, but here comes your soldier."

Anna grimaced. "I do not have a soldier."

"Uh-huh. That's why you get a funny look on your face when you're thinking about him. Not to mention the rosy color in your cheeks." Dottie shrugged. "Whatever he is, he's headed this way. And I need to get home. Call if you need anything."

"Thanks for the ride." Anna squeezed out a smile and

opened the car door. When she turned around, Sid stood there, a peaceful presence. She tapped down the irritation that mixed with a bewildering urge to run into his arms. "What are you doing here?"

"Nothing. Thought I'd come see if you need anything."

"I've told you we can't afford to pay the prisoners. Please take the men and leave." She fought the urge to cringe. Where had those harsh words come from?

His stance stiffened, and his eyes hardened at her words. "And I've reminded you that your father signed a contract with the county extension agent." Sid crossed his arms. "Until that contract is canceled, we'll keep coming."

"Wonderful. And what am I supposed to pay you with? Last year's leftover potatoes? The sugar beets nobody wants? No, I know. How about one of the cows we no longer own?" She sucked in a breath and held it a moment. "We don't have anything. And as long as Papa hides in the house, that won't change." She fought the beginnings of tears that tickled her throat. She would not cry in front of him. She crossed her arms and set her jaw.

Sid held up his hands, palms out. "Hey, I'm not the enemy. We're here to help. And if I could trust your father with the prisoners, I wouldn't come anymore."

The pain that assailed Anna at the thought of Sid not coming anymore took her breath away. Who would make sure she was okay each weekend? It wasn't his job, but he'd seemed to adopt her as one of his responsibilities. Or was it a duty? She cringed at the thought. She wasn't the duty of anyone—not even a soldier who cared for no reason at all other than he wanted to.

Anna opened her mouth, but the words froze in her throat. She must be more tired than she thought. The screen door slammed behind her. She turned to see Papa standing on the step, arms crossed, legs splayed, and back ramrod straight. Even from a hundred feet, she could see the tight set to his eyes.

"I have to go." Anna whispered the words. She reached to

pick up her bag and startled when Sid's fingers brushed hers.

"Let me carry that to the door for you."

Anna nodded and backed out of his way. She hurried toward the door without stopping to see if Sid followed. "Hi, Papa."

He looked at her with an expression that let her know she'd hear his thoughts soon. She hoped he'd wait until Sid returned to the prisoners. She grabbed his arm and pulled him into the house. Sid set the bag on the floor of the kitchen.

"Thank you."

Sid looked at her, eyebrow quirked in a question. She mouthed the word "Go," and he nodded. With a second look, he slipped out the door.

"What do you think you're doing, girlie?"

So much for waiting until Sid returned to the fields.

"I don't want you mixed up with some soldier. Especially one who fraternizes with the Germans."

"He doesn't fraternize. It's his job to guard them."

"Nobody should enjoy it as much as he does. Doesn't he remember they're the enemy? I don't like anyone who gets that friendly with them."

"What's this really about, Papa? The Germans in our fields? Or the war you fought in? And if you're so against it, why on earth did you sign a contract inviting them to be here?" Anna took a deep breath, trying to stem the rush of words that flooded her. "You know we have no way to pay them."

Papa glared at her, standing stiffly to his full height of six feet. Any other time, that could intimidate her, but Anna faced him squarely. He needed to answer some questions. Without answers, she didn't know how to proceed.

His jaw tightened.

"You don't have to answer, but I will talk to Specialist Chance. He's been nothing but kind to us from the first moment he stepped on this farm."

❧

Sid stared at the house from his vantage point by the barn. He rubbed at the knotted muscles in his neck. Why did he feel such an urge to protect Anna? There had to be more to it than his failure with Pattie. After all, Anna had handled her father fine for years without him.

Even as the thought came to him, he wondered if it was true. Had she really been safe, or had she lacked options? She had opportunities now yet chose to come home every weekend. He didn't know if he could do it with a dad like hers. The old codger could be mean. Though Sid had never seen the man get physical, he threatened more than any man should.

Why did Anna have to remind him so much of his sister? Every time he looked at her, he saw the bruises lining his sister's arms. That was a different situation. Pattie had made a poor choice in her husband. Anna's father wouldn't beat her. Fathers didn't do that. Not even grumpy, drunk old men like Ed Goodman. Right?

Even as Sid wanted to know the answer, he knew there was even less he could do for Anna than he'd done for Pattie. A woman had to desire freedom from the abuse. Otherwise, all of his intervention wouldn't mean a thing. She'd just return to the relationship.

He really should get back to the fields. Make sure the prisoners were on task. Yet he couldn't tear himself away from his post. He had to wait and ensure nothing happened between Anna and her father. Regardless of whether she wanted his help, she had it.

Until God released him from this burden for the Goodmans, he would be here as often as he could make his duties overlap with his concern.

No movement showed through the windows except a curtain flickering in a light breeze.

"Specialist Chance?"

The voice sounded like Luka's. He wouldn't call unless someone needed Sid. Sid looked at the house one more time.

Anna knew how to find him as long as he was here. He'd have to trust God with her safety. Surely God would hear and answer this prayer.

twelve

The days of June slipped away with a speed that left Anna wishing she could cling to each. The news that filtered out of Europe in the days after D-day left her with a tight feeling in her chest. Why hadn't they received word from Brent? Anna sat on her bed in the small bedroom she shared with Dottie, clutching the thin stack of letters she'd received from her brother since he shipped out. Several had thinned edges from constant reading. If only he would write more often. Answer each letter she sent to him. Even a short note that he'd survived the assault would be better than the silence that had dragged on for months.

As a pilot, wasn't he based at an airfield like Kearney? The post office here handled more than five thousand pieces of mail each day. Surely any base he lived on had similar facilities. Mail would come in and out unless Brent lived on the front lines. And that didn't make sense. Not for a member of a bomber crew.

Anna glanced at her Bible, resting on the chair next to her bed. She grabbed it and clutched it to her chest. *Father, I need some peace. And it has to come from You. Nothing else will get me through today.*

That prayer circled through her mind throughout the day. Something was wrong. She couldn't shake the cold grip on her heart no matter how often she prayed.

Later that morning as her needle passed through the silk fabric on a damaged plane wing, she wondered where her faith had gone. She used to believe that she could move mountains if she believed. Now her prayers didn't seem to pass any farther than the ceiling. Her faith must be much smaller than she had thought.

"Miss Goodman?"

Anna looked up to see Corporal Robertson standing in the doorway watching her with a closed expression. She glanced down at the wing in front of her. Had her fingers stopped working while she'd agonized? No, she'd continued to work.

"Please come with me."

Dottie shot her an encouraging smile as Anna followed Corporal Robertson. Anna tried to match it but failed. The grip on her heart tightened until she had to rub over the spot in an effort to ease the pain.

"Yes, sir?"

"You're wanted in the administration building."

"Any idea why?"

"I'm not at liberty to say."

Her fears for Brent disappeared as she tried to identify what infraction she'd committed to get called into the office. She double-timed to keep up with Colonel Robertson's long strides as they crossed the base. Too soon, they arrived at the office.

"Good luck, Miss Goodman."

Anna scanned his face, looking for any encouragement. All she found hiding in his eyes was a hint of compassion. Compassion? From Corporal Robertson? Anna tried to propel her feet to move, but they remained frozen to the sidewalk as if a sea of ice encased them.

Corporal Robertson watched a moment then opened the door for her.

"Thank you." Anna swallowed and entered the room.

Several desks were lined in shallow rows across the room. She watched the activity and wondered whom she should approach. Corporal Robertson could have given her some more information.

"Can I help you, miss?" A young woman from the far desk stood and approached Anna.

Anna's smile wavered. "Corporal Robertson told me to come here."

"Your name?"

"Anna Goodman." She'd choke if someone didn't tell her what was going on. Soon.

"Oh. Please come with me." The young woman escorted Anna to a door next to the office. Anna felt huge compared to her escort's dainty form that wasn't hidden under a bulky pair of coveralls. The thought of working in an office hadn't appealed to Anna before. Now she wondered if the guys wouldn't be more interested if she looked feminine each day instead of wearing her work uniform.

She stopped. Where had that thought come from? Since when did she care about what men thought about her? Especially when the job she did was important to the war effort?

Maybe she'd eaten something funny yesterday and that's why everything seemed out of kilter. Surely she'd worked herself up over nothing.

"Right this way."

Anna startled. The gal held open the door. Anna approached the door and looked inside. Sid stood there, hat in his hands, shoulders bowed as if under some great load.

"Sid, what's wrong? Did something happen to Papa?" The words tumbled over each other as she ran into the room. "Please tell me he's okay." He might be insufferable some days, but he was all she had left. *Please, God.*

Sid reached out to steady her. "He's okay. He asked me to get you when I dropped off the prisoners today."

Anna searched his eyes, desperate to believe him. But his words did not change the reality that something was wrong. If all was fine, Sid wouldn't be standing in front of her now.

"You need to come back with me, Anna. He wouldn't tell me anything other than it's an emergency."

She nodded then followed him to a Jeep.

After driving for ten minutes in silence, Sid thumped the wheel. "Anna, how would you like to accompany me to dinner on Saturday? We could slip into one of the USOs or attend a show some prisoners are putting on for the officers at Camp Atlanta. Some of those have been pretty good."

Anna tried to pull her mind from the fears tangoing around. "All right. I can do that."

"Come on. Don't make it sound like it's a chore." He took his eyes off the road for a second to pull a face at her. "You might even have a good time. It's okay to relax, you know."

"Make it Friday night. I'd like that." Her fingers twisted the handles of her purse as she tried to focus on their date rather than on the unknown that awaited her at home.

The rest of the ride passed in a silent blur. Anna couldn't calm her thoughts that spiraled in a myriad of directions before returning to a central fear. Something was wrong. If Papa was okay, then something had happened to Brent. What would Papa have to live for if her fears were true?

Before she'd prepared herself, Sid pulled the truck in front of her house. Anna stared out the window at the home that now stood like nothing more than a shell. Mere walls constructed of wood and covered by a roof. The heart of love had died.

She needed to get out of the vehicle. March into the house. Face head-on whatever awaited her.

And all she could do was sit there like a statue. Trapped by her fears.

"Do you want me to come in with you?"

She started to nod then stopped herself. She couldn't depend on Sid. Maybe Papa was right about him. He remained a soldier who'd disappear like the rest when new orders arrived.

"No. I'll be fine."

"You don't have to face this alone."

Yes, she did. That was her life. One disaster after another to handle without help or support. She turned to open the door, but Sid hopped out and ran around the truck. He swung the door open and offered his hand.

"I'm praying for you. God can help you through whatever waits in there." Sid nodded toward the house. He chucked her under the chin then stilled. Her breath caught at the intensity in his eyes. His gaze trailed to her mouth then back up. He stepped back, but his gaze continued to pierce through to her soul. "Let me help. I won't push, but I'm not disappearing, either."

How had he read her thoughts? Anna sucked in a breath, ordered her heart to calm down. Now wasn't the time to act like a schoolgirl. She let him help her down then released his hand.

"Thank you for the ride." She closed her eyes and prayed for strength to accept whatever lay inside that door.

Slowed by dread, Anna climbed the steps to the door and pushed through.

"Papa, I'm home." Her words echoed in the stillness.

She walked from the kitchen to the living room, but Papa didn't recline in his favorite chair. She looked back into the kitchen, expecting to find that she'd overlooked him at the table.

"Papa?" Her tone rose as she continued to call for him. Anna slipped down the hall to his bedroom. The door was closed, but she knocked anyway. "I'm here like you asked, Papa. Please let me in."

The silence dragged on so long that she feared he'd slipped out of the house.

"Anna?"

Her knees trembled from relief. She twisted the knob and eased the door open. "Yes?"

Papa's face sagged under the weight of new wrinkles that had appeared in the couple of days since she'd returned to Kearney. A tremor shook his hand as he reached for her. She stilled. When had he last reached out to her? Tears welled in her eyes.

"What is it? Please, you have to tell me."

He reached for a yellow paper on the bedside table. Anna ran to the bed and sank beside it as she grabbed the thin slip of paper. Her mind refused to absorb the simple message:

REGRET TO REPORT YOUR SON BRENT GOODMAN IS MISSING IN ACTION OVER FRANCE.

Anna sucked in a shuddering breath then tried to read the words again through tears that streamed down her cheeks. She looked up to find tears trickling down Papa's cheeks. He reached for her, and she leaned into his embrace.

She tried to absorb the news and cling to the hope that he wasn't confirmed dead. Surely there was hope in that.

But reality wouldn't release her from its grip. Brent served on a B-17. If his plane had gone down, he'd either died or become a prisoner.

She clung to Papa. What was left to fight for? Brent. Until the army changed his status from MIA to KIA, she would fight for the farm. He would need somewhere to return to when he came home.

And she would fight to keep Papa from disappearing inside himself during this latest battle.

She had to, or she was afraid she'd join him in his pit of despair.

thirteen

Sid eyed his reflection in the mirror. He looked standard military issue. Nothing that stood out in a crowd, unless you counted his slightly off-center nose. It had never recovered from that fight during basic training.

He straightened his tie and splashed some cologne on his neck. Time to collect Anna.

He hopped into Trent's Ford. It wasn't Cinderella's carriage, not with as many years as it had run up and down the roads. Neither was it a government-issued truck. He wanted tonight to feel like a special event. Wanted to focus on getting to know her beyond the surface level of their interactions on the farm. When he caught her away from the farm, she delighted him with her stories and wit. Only on the farm did they have confrontations rather than conversations.

Tuesday when he'd invited her, it had seemed like the right thing to do. She'd agreed without much reluctance. Now if she could muster up a bit of excitement, the night could be great.

Sid whistled as he drove the few miles from Camp Atlanta to the Goodman farm.

As he ran to the door, Sid wondered what had happened after he'd dropped Anna off Tuesday. He'd waited as long as he could before taking the prisoners back to camp. The poor men had looked wrung out from their day in the fields. And Sid couldn't tell if the fields had benefited from their labor. They'd returned the next day, and he'd monitored the men carefully, pleased with their progress. The only disappointment came when he learned that Anna had returned to Kearney early that morning. How had she made it back?

Now he knocked on the door, a grin he couldn't restrain spreading across his face.

The door opened, and Mr. Goodman stared at him.

"Good evening, sir. I'm here for Anna."

The man grunted a reply.

"Is she ready?"

"I don't like the idea of my girl going out with you."

Sid felt the edges of his grin fall. The sound of footsteps running reached his ears.

"If this fool girl'd listen to me at all, she'd stay right here where she belongs rather than run around with a soldier who's just gonna get killed."

Heat flamed up Sid's neck as Mr. Goodman yelled. He tried to swallow the urge to explode; then he caught a glimpse of Anna. Her face had turned white as snow, and her mouth hung open.

"Papa!" Anna sputtered as if trying to catch a breath. "That's enough."

"No, you need to hear all this. Maybe it'll sink in this time. Spend time with a man in uniform, and he'll break your heart. If your mama still lived, she'd tell you that exact thing." Mr. Goodman's voice broke on the last sentence, and then he caught himself. He thrust his finger in Sid's face, forcing Sid down a stair. "You leave my girl alone."

Sid looked from Mr. Goodman to Anna, unsure what to do. Should he leave? Or should he fight for the right to take Anna out for an evening? What did Anna want? He searched her face but found nothing in her blank expression to indicate her desires.

He balanced on the balls of his feet while he waited for whatever Mr. Goodman would throw his way next.

"Papa, please let me through." Anna's voice barely reached Sid's ears yet held strength. "Mama told me she loved you and never for one moment regretted marrying a soldier. She would encourage me to spend time with a man like Sid. Especially after the way he's cared for the farm."

Uh-oh. Now Sid could feel the heat climb to include his ears. Marriage? He only wanted to spend an evening with Anna. Not the rest of his life. At least not until he knew her better. A lot better. He ran a finger under his collar. Maybe he should leave now. Before someone said anything else that would make his temperature rise higher.

Mr. Goodman sighed and stepped back. "Don't say I didn't warn you. And remember what happened to your brother."

"How can I forget?" Anna slipped past her father to Sid's side. "Take me away, soldier."

He held out his arm, and she grabbed it like a lifeline. He felt her hand tremble against him, and he covered it with his own. "Are you sure you want to go?"

She bit her lip and nodded, her gaze on the ground in front of her.

A snort behind him made Sid turn. Mr. Goodman remained in the doorway, watching them like a hawk.

"Don't look back."

"Why?"

"He'll take pleasure from knowing you care what he's doing. Papa's become a great manipulator in the last couple of years."

Sid opened the car's door and helped Anna in. He walked around the car and slid behind the wheel. "Let me make a suggestion. Since you still want to spend the evening with me, let's drive to Holdrege and the diner there. After that, if we have time, we can go to Camp Atlanta for the prisoners' show or for a movie. Or we can stay in Holdrege for a dance in the park. Whichever sounds good to you."

Anna sniffled. Sid felt a spike of alarm course through him. No, not a woman crying. Anything but that! He glanced at her, but she turned toward the door.

"So you don't like my plan. That's okay." Sid reached for something, anything that would distract her. If only he knew what had set her off. Where had his wit disappeared when he needed it? "How about a trip to Kearney?"

A sniffle answered him.

"Or a trip to Omaha. We could really make your dad crazy with the idea we ran off and eloped." Did he just say that?

She sniffled again, and a tiny giggle escaped. Okay, this was working.

"I know. How about a run south? We could slip into Kansas and drive until we hit Mexico. I'm sure no one would miss us. We could pretend you were a princess and I'm your escort whisking you away to a magical world."

A watery laugh filled the car. "No, let's drive west until we hit the mountains. We can find a corner of Colorado no one's claimed. Pretend the world is simpler."

"Or we could go into Holdrege and have dinner."

From the side he watched Anna's cheeks curve. "I'd like that. It'll work until we can run away without the military chasing you across the country."

Sid waved her off. "No worries. What's one lowly specialist in a sea of enlisted men? I am the one who lost the prisoner, after all. I'm sure they'd find my disappearance a huge loss."

"Surely they've forgotten."

He thought of the pranks that dogged his steps. "It's probably written up in my file. My kids will someday discover the wonderful fact that their daddy lost a German. In rural Nebraska." He heaved a sigh. "The price of notoriety."

Anna wiped her eyes, and a comfortable silence filled the car. They reached the outskirts of Holdrege, and Sid watched the small homes whiz past. Soon he turned the car onto Main Street. It wasn't long, and most of the businesses looked shuttered. Fortunately, Rosy's Diner blazed with light. He made a big show of inhaling.

"Smell her famous biscuits?"

Anna followed suit and started coughing. "All I smell is exhaust."

"Then we'd better get you inside. Can't have something happen to you on my watch."

"No. Wouldn't want to become like the prisoner."

He nearly choked as she scampered out of the car and up to the café.

"Come on, slowpoke."

Her emotions had definitely improved. He shook his head. What was it with women and feelings that changed like the weather? He'd get whiplash around her if he didn't watch out.

Soon he had Anna settled at a table tucked in a corner halfway between the door and the kitchen. Stains dotted the once-white tablecloth, but the lit candle in the middle of the table pulled his attention to Anna's eyes. While a smile now touched her lips, it didn't reach her eyes. Shadows filled them.

They talked for a few minutes before the waitress came for their order. After she left, Sid placed his hand over Anna's.

"Will you tell me what's wrong?"

Anna looked away, scanning the room as if for an escape. "What do you mean?"

"Something more than your father has you distracted."

She tugged her hand free from his. A mask settled over her features, and he wished he could retract the question. Then again, maybe not. Someone needed to climb beneath the surface with her. See what caused the hurt that shadowed her expression.

An awkward silence fell between them until, finally, the waitress placed their plates in front of them. "Can I get you anything else?"

Sid shook his head, and she sashayed away.

"Can I pray before we eat?"

Anna nodded without a word.

"Father, join us tonight. I ask You to comfort Anna. You know her inside and out. Please give her whatever she needs tonight. Amen."

She eyed him and then picked up her silverware. "Do you always pray like that?"

"Only when I don't know what else to say or do."

"Hmm." She took a bite of her vegetables and chewed.

"We had a telegram Tuesday."

Sid looked up, trying to read her expression. Telegrams rarely contained good news anymore. "What did it say?"

Tears ran down her cheeks. He reached across the table with his napkin and wiped one away.

"Brent's missing in action. The military probably presumes he's dead. It likely happened with the assault on Normandy."

He longed to take her into his arms and hold her until everything was okay.

"I'm sorry Papa turned so mean when you came tonight. He wants to protect me. All I want is Brent home with us."

She buried her face in her hands as her shoulders shook. Sid noticed those at the tables around them starting to stare. "Would you like me to get you out of here?"

A nod indicated she'd heard him. He strode to the cash register at the front of the dining room and handed over some cash and ration coupons.

"Want me to package your meals?"

Sid glanced at the table where Anna sat wiping her face. "Yes. Thanks."

The waitress wrapped up the fried chicken and sides, then handed the containers to him. Once he had Anna in the car, she leaned against the seat and closed her eyes.

He reached to crank the engine then stopped. "What would you like to do now? Go somewhere to talk or back home?"

"Take me to the park."

Sid drove to the park and came to a stop at the edge of the lot for the dance.

"Have you ever felt like God abandoned you?"

The quiet question filled the car like a bomb exploding. Sid prayed for an answer but remained quiet.

"Why is God so mad at me? He's stripping everything away from me. First Mama. Now Brent." She curled into herself against the door of the car. "I haven't done anything to deserve this. All I know is every time I try to hold things together, something else gets pulled away. I'm ready to stop trying altogether." Her hand covered her mouth as if stifling any more words.

Sid turned toward Anna. What could he say to penetrate the walls of hurt? Should he say anything? Silence settled over the car, and Anna turned to him before he could formulate anything profound.

"Please take me home now." Her voice shook.

He looked at her, smelling the fried chicken, and tried to read whether she really wanted to go home. Her features were shuttered. He'd missed an opportunity she might not hand him again, but he had to try. "Look, let's go sit over there on the bench and eat our dinner. The moon's out, and it's a beautiful night. If you want to go home after that, I'll take you."

She nodded. He hurried out of the car and around to open her door before she could change her mind. "Here you go, m'lady."

"Thank you." She leaned into him as they walked to a bench. He held her tight against him with one arm while he juggled their meals with the other.

"Here's the bench," he said, easing her down to it. He handed her the container holding her meal and then watched as she picked at the meat. After the first bite, she ate her portion quickly. Sid wiped his mouth on a napkin then turned to her. "I'm sorry about everything that's happened, Anna. I wish I could fix this. All I can promise is that I'm here if you ever need me."

She snuggled closer and nodded. "I know. Can you take me home now?"

As he drove her home, he sensed her trying to push him away. She couldn't so easily distance herself. Somehow he'd find the way into her heart.

fourteen

The strains of "Swinging on a Star" filtered through the parachute room. Anna had stopped counting how many the army could cram into the room at a time, but in the late June heat, the room felt stifling. She wiped a trail of sweat off her forehead with one hand while keeping a firm grip on the lines she'd untangled with the other.

News continued to trickle from the front in Europe. Now when shipments of fresh B-17s were matched with their crews from Kearney, the air of celebration was gone. These men would fly straight into Europe and the fight.

She wavered between reminders that Brent had disappeared, likely presumed dead, and the thought that while she couldn't help him, she could help these men. She stifled a yawn. She slept fitfully. The smell of food turned her stomach. All she wanted to do was curl up in a corner and hide from the world. Instead, she plugged on because that's what Goodmans did—or what they'd done until her father decided to distance himself from life.

Chin up, Anna. Goodmans always face their troubles head-on.

How many times had he said those words when it looked like they'd lose the farm? The war had started, and things had looked up until Brent enlisted. Then Mama died. And now Brent was missing.

Dottie walked to her and stood like a shield between Anna and the rest of the room. "Are you okay?"

"Yes. Why?"

"You might want to wipe the tears off your cheeks."

Anna touched her face. "I didn't realize I'd started crying."

"I know. Finish that parachute, and let's take a break."

As Dottie and Anna walked back from their coffee break,

Anna's gaze landed on the chapel. Something about the simple white structure drew her.

"I'm going to stop in there."

"Take your time. I'll cover for you." Dottie squeezed Anna's hand then continued toward the repair hangar.

Anna stood still, looking at the chapel. She'd passed the building numerous times yet never felt this urge to walk inside. "Just for a minute." The stacks of tangled parachutes called to her, but maybe she could give her full attention to the job after spending a few moments soaking in the quiet of this place.

She pulled open the door and slipped into the foyer. It took her eyes a moment to adjust to the dim interior. Anna hesitated. Now that she stood in the building, she didn't know what to do. No sense of peace enveloped her. No presence whispered hope to her soul. She felt just as empty here as she did anywhere else. The questions, the sense of abandonment that followed her through the days and nights, still lingered. Trailing her hand along the backs of the pews, Anna walked to the front and sank onto one. The windows were simple, without stained glass to delight the eyes.

"What do You want from me, God?" The words bounced off the wooden floors and carved pews. "Haven't You taken enough?"

She jumped up and pounded toward the altar. "You've taken Mama. Brent. Might as well have taken Papa. The land's left, but there's no money to keep it. Nobody to run it."

Is that true?

The words whispered in her soul, generating even more questions.

Different images filtered through Anna's mind like snapshots, many of them filled with people. Brent chasing her around the barn during morning chores years ago. The Wisdoms and the warm way they'd opened their home and hearts to her. Dottie and her solid friendship through the ups and downs. German prisoners laboring their hardest in the fields. Gus and Teddy laughing with her papa at the table. The pastor standing in front of the church, expounding on Sunday mornings. Sid watching over her and the farm.

She took a deep breath. Okay, maybe she hadn't been abandoned. Then why did she feel so. . .empty. . .isolated. . . drained?

Words from Sunday's sermon filled her mind. Pastor Reynolds had examined Deuteronomy 31 and the principle that God will not fail or forsake His people. He'd set a specific job in front of the Israelites but had promised to go with them. And because of that, the Israelites were to walk in courage and strength.

What was the job God had for her? At the moment, she wasn't doing anything well. So many different things pulled on her for time and attention. She couldn't pretend to handle it all anymore.

Good.

Good? How could it be good that she couldn't manage everything in front of her?

Rest in Me. I'll provide as I did for the Israelites.

The thought soaked into her heart. Maybe she didn't have to carry the burden alone. God could provide everything she needed. She certainly hadn't done a good job on her own.

Anna tipped her head toward heaven and lifted her hands. "Okay, Father. I don't even know if I can do this, but help me turn my fears and anxiety to You. Here's Brent. Take care of him if he's still alive. Help him find his way back to us." She shuddered and covered her face with her hands. She took a deep breath. She had to do this. "And here's Papa. Help me, Lord. I don't understand everything that's going on in him. But I know my life is meaningless without You."

The sound of footsteps echoed off the wood floors. Anna lowered her hands and turned to find a man approaching her.

"Can I help you?" Though hooded with fatigue, his eyes crinkled at the edges. Peace radiated from his gaze.

"Is it okay that I came in?"

"It's why I leave the doors unlocked. Come anytime." He settled onto the pew next to her and stared at the simple cross behind the pulpit. "I've been thinking about the evening service."

Anna tried to look interested. Where was he headed?

"I spend much of my time talking to different soldiers and airmen. Do you know what their biggest concern is?"

She shook her head as a list filled her mind. Fear of the unknown? Concern for those they left behind? Apprehension about doing their jobs well? The list seemed endless.

"For those who have faith, they want to know that God will go with them into battle. For others, it's fear of death. What wonderful assurance that God promises never to leave us even when He sends us into battle." He leaned against the pew. "That's an amazing promise. Now if we could learn how to live like we believed it." He studied her closely. "That's the challenge I have. To present that truth in such a way that it transforms lives."

The bell on top of the chapel tolled out the new hour. Anna eased from the pew. Time to get back to work. Time to see if she could live. Time to see if she'd relinquished her fears. Like that promise was hers. She needed God to go with her in order to survive the battles with her father. An uneasiness filled her that Papa would take out all his pent-up rage on the prisoners someday. Having them at the farm brought out the worst in him. She needed to talk to Sid about that before something happened.

"Good luck with your sermon."

The chaplain smiled at her. "Remember, the door is always unlocked."

"Thank you." She returned his smile then walked down the aisle and out the chapel.

Anna wound back to the repair hangar. She took her time, since she'd already missed an hour. For the first time in a while, she noticed the base around her. Outside one administrative building, someone had taken the time to plant a flower bed. Purple coneflowers mixed with pure white daisies. Honeybees buzzed between the plants, collecting the precious nectar.

Soldiers and civilians raced past her, but for once she didn't join them. A bomber crew walked by. One of the group wolf-whistled, and she nodded in acknowledgment but didn't stop. He must be desperate if he thought she was attractive in her work garb.

She and God had a few issues to work through. Then, maybe, she would be ready to consider a relationship with someone. But it wouldn't be with someone who whistled indiscriminately.

No, it would be someone who made her feel sheltered and protected.

Someone like Sid.

fifteen

The fields that lined the road showed the benefit of rain. Winter wheat stood ready to harvest in another week to ten days. The corn reached toward the sky, feet yet to grow but well on its way. Even the neighbors' soybeans had started to take on their bunched forms.

Sid braced himself for the conflict he would walk into when he reached the Goodman farm. Not the way he'd planned to end his week. However, the wheat needed to be harvested in a matter of days, but Mr. Goodman had refused to pay the prisoners. The county extension officer shifted on the seat next to him.

"Are you sure I need to be here?" Jude Rosen looked as uncomfortable as a hen surrounded by foxes.

"Last time I checked, your job as county agent included collecting the prisoners' wages. I transport them."

"But I told you Ed Goodman won't see me. Last time he threw me out."

"That's why I'm here. Think of me as your protection."

Jude scrunched down in his seat. Sid thought he might have to pull him from the military Jeep. "Look, this farm will go under if we don't get this resolved. The wheat crop will rot in the fields without prisoner labor. You know it, and I know it. Mr. Goodman will before we leave."

"You haven't known him as long as I have. That man is more stubborn than the most obnoxious bull."

Sid decided he'd take Jude at his word. He had no desire to test that theory. But the Goodman farm would be in serious trouble if the crop didn't get out of the fields. Then came the corn, but that wouldn't be ready to harvest until the end of October at the earliest. One battle at a time.

The two men approached the house, and Sid couldn't detect any signs of life. He knocked on the door and waited for any sound to indicate that Mr. Goodman headed their way to answer it. After a minute, he rapped again.

"Well, guess he doesn't want to talk to us." Jude headed toward the Jeep.

"You can't leave without me, so you might as well stick around and do your job." Sid stood firm as a storm passed over Jude's face.

He shook a finger in Sid's face. "Do you understand how mean that man can be?"

If only Jude knew that Sid had found Mr. Goodman holding the prisoner at gunpoint. Or how many arguments he'd overheard. Yep, he had a good sense of the bile in that man's mind.

Sid reached out and knocked again. "We'll leave when we know Mr. Goodman isn't here."

A moment later, the door flew open. "What do you think you want?" Mr. Goodman stood in the doorway in his undershirt and jeans, a scowl plastered across his face.

Jude stood slack-jawed in front of the man. Sid elbowed him then took over when Jude remained frozen. "We're here to discuss the farm labor you've used this year."

"What about it?"

"You're behind in payments, and the prisoners can't return until you're current."

"So?"

"You have anybody else lined up to help with harvest? Planning to do it on your own? One man and a plow?" Sid tried to keep the derision from his voice. The man might not be an honorable man at the moment, but he'd heard enough stories to know Mr. Goodman hadn't always lived like this.

Mr. Goodman crossed his arms and stared at Sid. "Now why would I pay for Nazi labor? I think they've taken enough from me."

"You don't know Brent's dead."

"Maybe, but he's either dead or a prisoner. And you can bet they ain't treating him as soft as you treat the prisoners."

"The Geneva Convention applies to the Germans, too, sir."

"You didn't fight in the last war. Mark my words: We're too good to these prisoners." He spat out the final word. "We're done."

Sid pushed against the door to keep it from closing. "No. You need the men for the harvest."

"I'll make that girl of mine come home."

"She wouldn't know what to do even if you made her come home. Did you ever teach her how to harvest with a team?"

"Well, no." Mr. Goodman looked away. "She's always helped around, but not helped with the actual farming."

"I know she's a smart gal, but you'll need able-bodied men if the wheat's to get harvested in time."

Mr. Goodman turned from the door and hurried deeper into the house. Sid stared after him, wondering if he should follow.

Jude stepped inside. "Guess he wants us to follow him."

The two made themselves at home at the kitchen table. Mr. Goodman returned from down the hall and threw a coffee can at Jude. Jude fumbled with it a moment.

"What am I supposed to do with this? It feels empty."

"Look inside." Mr. Goodman stood rigidly in front of them, a taut expression on his face. "That is the sum of cash I have. That's it. All I have to get me through until I sell the crops. It's earmarked for taxes, not that either of you care."

All at once, Sid realized the man in front of him stood broken. Life had overwhelmed, and in his mind, he'd done all he could and still lost. No wonder he acted defeated all the time and took it out on anyone who had the misfortune of getting near him. Sid watched Jude count the money. "How close is he?"

"About two dollars short."

"But close enough, right?"

"Sure." Jude looked as though all he cared about was

leaving the house in one piece.

"Thanks, Mr. Goodman. I'll have my best group here in a week to start the harvest." Sid stood and offered his hand to the man. After a reluctant shake, Mr. Goodman nodded. "We'll leave you alone now. Have a good evening."

Jude hustled out of the kitchen and to the Jeep. Sid climbed in and turned the Jeep around but had to stop as another car drove down the lane. He stilled then looked at his watch. It was only four o'clock, early for Dottie to drop Anna off. Even as his heartbeat surged, he had to admit he'd scheduled the trip out here for now, hoping to see her even for a few minutes.

Anna climbed out of the car, and Jude sighed. "Guess we won't be going anywhere soon."

"Why?"

"The reason you're so concerned about the farm isn't Mr. Goodman. Nope, it's that lovely young lady over there." He gestured to where Anna stood watching his Jeep, a smile on her lips.

Sid shrugged. Why deny the truth? "Maybe you can get a ride to town with Dottie. I'm sure she wouldn't mind." Sid couldn't leave before he knew everything was okay with Anna and her father.

❧

Anna's heart raced in her chest as if she'd run the length of the farm with a message. How could the sight of Sid Chance do that to her? Her eyes drank in the sight of him while her feet refused to move.

"Go on. I can't leave until you step away from my wheels." Laughter livened Dottie's words.

"How can I be so mad at a man and so drawn to him at the same time?" Anna sighed and leaned against the car. "I am such a mess."

"I do believe most people call it flashes of love."

Anna snorted. "That is the last thing I would call what I feel toward him. Animosity. Friendship, maybe."

"And it's natural to hate someone you're friends with?

When you're ready to admit the truth, I'll try not to tell you I told you so."

The horn honked, and Anna jerked away from the car. "You didn't need to do that."

"Maybe not, but it was fun. Don't forget I need to pick you up tomorrow night."

"I'll be ready."

Dottie climbed behind the wheel then muttered, "Looks like I didn't leave soon enough."

Jude Rosen strode toward the car. His face hung long like that of a condemned soldier.

Dottie climbed out of the car and nailed him with a glare. "Let me guess. You think you'll ride with me." At his miserable nod, she snorted. "Hop in if you're brave enough."

They pulled out of the drive, and Anna shook her head. "I hope they both survive the trip to town."

Sid stood next to her, arms crossed even as he stood at ease. "Why do you say that?"

"There's a lot of history between those two, and none of it's good. Surely you had a good reason to put them together."

"Jude and I came out to collect the wages your dad owed."

Heat crept up Anna's face. Times like this she wished her skin was bronzed by the sun to better hide her flashes of emotion. "I told you we didn't have the money."

"He came close, though he wasn't happy about it. Pulled out a can filled with cash."

"That money should pay the taxes." Anna stamped her foot. "Do you know how hard it is to get cash money? Farmers don't get a steady salary like you soldiers. No, we have to scrimp and save every penny we find, because who knows when the next will arrive? First the Depression. Then the Dust Bowl. Now things begin to improve, and Papa stops working."

"He had to pay." The muscles tightened in Sid's face as he spoke. "If he didn't, I couldn't bring prisoners here to harvest the winter wheat. What's your plan? Hitch that old mare to the wagon and do it all yourself? I don't see a tractor around here to help with the work."

"Of course not. A tractor takes money. Lots of it." Anna swallowed hard against the lump that had developed in her throat. She would not cry in front of this insolent man. She looked around, desperate for an escape.

Sid placed a hand on her shoulder. The gentle action nearly undid her.

"I'm not the enemy. I'm trying to help."

Anna nodded, not trusting herself to speak. She stared at Sid's hand on her shoulder, wanting desperately to shake it off, distance herself from him before he got too close. Saw how scared she was. How isolated she felt.

Sid stepped away, taking his support. He shoved his hands in his pockets and looked at her as if he could see right through her. Anna stiffened and raised her chin. She would not let him in that far.

"Look. Be careful when you go inside. I'm not sure what kind of mood your dad will be in. He seemed sober when we left, but that was twenty minutes ago."

Anna rolled her eyes. Surely he hadn't returned to that tired path.

"Fine. Consider yourself warned." Sid took a breath and glanced around the farm. "July Fourth is coming up."

"Yes." Where was he headed?

"Why don't you and Dottie, and any other gals who would like to, come down and join us at Camp Atlanta? We're having a big celebration."

Why on earth would she spend more time with this overly opinionated soldier who had no shortage of ideas about how she and Papa should live their lives? "I'd like that. I'll see if Dottie can join me." Anna shut her mouth before any other unintended commitments escaped. What would she say if he asked her to marry him right now? She shuddered at the thought.

Sid stood tall, a grin slapped across his face. "That's great. I'll call you at the Wisdoms on Monday to confirm details.

I think the camp is sending a bus to Kearney to collect folks. See you then."

Anna watched him stride to the Jeep, wondering what on earth she'd agreed to.

sixteen

July 4, 1944

Someone pounded on the bedroom door, and Anna stirred. Dottie mumbled something in her sleep and rolled over. The twin bed creaked in time with her movements. Anna pulled the blanket over her head and tried to slip back to sleep.

"Anna, you have a call."

Anna flopped over and grabbed the alarm clock from the bedside table. Five thirty. What was so important at this hour of the morning? The night had passed slowly as she tossed and turned from dream to dream. Papa, Brent, even Sid took turns starring.

The pounding echoed off the door.

"We're up." Anna slid out of bed and grabbed her robe. Her thoughts flashed to the last time someone had woken them up. The war couldn't be over already, could it? Talk about wishful thinking. She pulled open the door. "Mr. Wisdom. What's wrong?"

"Phone's for you, Anna." His brow crinkled in apparent concern as he spoke.

"Thank you." She slipped out of the room and followed him down the hallway and stairwell. The family's phone stood in the kitchen. Anna took a deep breath and braced herself before picking it up. The news couldn't be good this early in the morning. "Hello? This is Anna."

"It's about time."

"Good morning, Papa."

"I don't know what's good about it." Though his words were gruff, she heard something in his voice that made her wait. "I couldn't find your number last night. Really hid that, didn't you?"

Anna rolled her eyes. She had pasted the Wisdoms number in Mama's old address book. "Sorry. Why call this early in the morning?" Especially when she couldn't think of a single other time he'd called.

"Well, I thought you'd like to know Gus and Teddy came for dinner last night."

Were his words slurred, or were her ears merely tired? Anna hated the fact that between her fears and Sid's accusations, she analyzed every nuance of Papa's speech patterns. Maybe he'd always rolled his *r*'s, and she hadn't noticed.

"I'm glad to hear that, Papa. Is there anything else?" If he got off the phone soon, maybe she could get a few more minutes of sleep before heading to work. And she still had to pack a change of clothes for the celebration at Camp Atlanta.

"Are you listening to me? I told you I had folks over. Thought you'd be more enthusiastic than that after your harping about getting on with living."

"You're right. I'm not used to getting wakened for a phone call."

"If you were home where you belong, you'd already be up and the cow milked."

"But I'm here, Papa. Doing my part for the war. Saving men's lives."

"And when was the last time you did that?"

The sound of her pulse filled her ears at his challenge. Why did he have to be so mean?

"Before you go back for your beauty sleep, you should know I got another military telegram."

Anna's heart stopped, and she rubbed her chest where it ached. She opened her mouth to ask what it said but couldn't get the words out.

"It's about your brother."

A gasp escaped Anna's throat. Her knees quivered, and she grabbed the counter.

"He's alive, thanks for asking. But he's a prisoner of the Germans in some place I can't pronounce."

The sense of relief fled at his words. A prisoner? Anna covered her mouth with a hand to stifle her tears. Papa was too upset to deal with her grief.

"You listening, girl?" His gruff voice ground into her ear.

She nodded then cleared her throat. "Yes, Papa. You're sure he's alive?"

The rustle of paper sifted across the line. "That's what it says here."

"That's better than we feared."

"Maybe, but he's a prisoner. Of the Nazis. They don't coddle the prisoners like we do." He snorted. "We treat the Germans too well."

"Papa." Anna pushed warning into her voice. He didn't need to think that way again. She didn't want to think what he'd do if he let that thought develop. "Tell me about dinner. And where are you calling me from?"

"Thought it was too early to bother you with details like that."

"I'm awake now. Who did the cooking?"

Papa harrumphed. "I did, and then made them clean. I've got to get to the chores. Bye."

Before Anna could respond, he'd hung up. She replaced the handset but didn't let go. "I wonder how many neighbors listened to that exchange."

"Everything all right, Anna?"

She startled and turned to find Mr. Wisdom leaning against the doorframe, concern filling his gray eyes. "Yes. Sorry he woke you. Papa wanted me to know Brent is no longer missing. The Germans captured him."

"Need anything?"

Anna swallowed and then shook her head. "I'll be fine."

"I'll let Mrs. Wisdom know."

"Thank you. And thank you for waking me." Anna dredged up a smile and slipped past him and up the stairs. When she entered the room, Dottie sat in the middle of her bed. She opened her arms, and Anna slid next to her.

"Brent's a prisoner."

"I'd ask if you'll be okay, but I know the answer to that."

Anna stared at her, unsure if she knew the answer.

"You'll walk around in shock for a day; then you'll square your shoulders, pray for Brent, and get back to work." Dottie squeezed Anna. "So here's the question. Are you working today and going to Camp Atlanta?"

Anna rubbed her hands together, trying to warm them, as she considered the question. "I can't do anything for Brent moping. I think the distraction will help."

"That's my best friend. You'll be happier if you're doing something." Dottie bounced out of bed and grabbed a bar of soap and a towel. "I'll go get cleaned up first."

Anna watched her go and pondered her words. She'd always had to carry on. Bear the load for other people. Now she couldn't do anything for Brent. Nothing but worry or pray. Somehow, she'd pray and release him.

The morning passed slowly as Anna let the other gals' babble flow around her. She couldn't make herself care about how hard it was to buy food, even with ration coupons. Or that Darling's Shoe Shop had received a shipment this week. Instead, she kept a constant prayer running through her mind—first thanking God that Brent was still alive, then asking why he had to be a prisoner. She knew to the core of her being that Papa was right. The Germans wouldn't treat him as well as all the prisoners at Atlanta were treated. But God could still protect him.

At two, Dottie and Anna joined the rest of the gals heading to Atlanta. A bus waited for them outside the gates. Anna ran a hand down the front of her navy skirt, almost expecting to feel the rougher material of her coveralls. She'd brushed out her curls and tried to freshen her face but had a feeling Sid would see right through her. The thought made her feel exposed.

The forty-three-mile trip passed in a blur of chatter. The other girls seemed excited about the chance to attend the celebration.

"I heard they're having fireworks, too." A cute redhead bounced on her seat.

"And a cookout with all the trimmings." Another gal licked her lips. "I can taste the hamburger now. The military doesn't have rationing, you know."

Anna tried to join into their excitement but didn't care about the food.

The chaperone, a thin, tired-looking woman in her forties, stood at the front of the bus as it approached the gates to Camp Atlanta. "Now remember, ladies, we are here as guests. Find a lonely soldier and help him join in the fun. Make conversation. Do not leave with a soldier, but stay with the group. Also, be mindful that the bus will leave at the close of the fireworks show. No lollygagging.

"Most of all, remember to have fun. If you do, the boys will, too."

The bus pulled to a stop, and Anna scanned the men assembled outside the bus. It didn't take long to spot Sid. He stood slightly to the side with his hat in his hands. He wore his dress uniform and looked very handsome. Why would he bother with her? Someday she needed to ask him. As she watched his face light up when he saw her, she decided today she'd enjoy the reality. For whatever reason, he'd decided to become her friend. And for today, she'd overlook the way he inserted himself with Papa. Today she wanted to forget about the farm and family burdens and pretend for a moment she was like these other girls. Here to have a good time, without a care to weigh her down.

Sid rushed up to her. "Hey, beautiful."

"Hello."

"Ready to enjoy the celebration? You look tired."

"Papa called this morning. The army located Brent in a German camp."

Sid picked her up and spun her around. She tried to catch her breath as he squeezed her tight.

"That's fantastic news, Anna."

"Yes, it's wonderful to know he's alive. I just wish he wasn't a prisoner." Anna straightened her skirt then glanced up at Sid. "Thanks for inviting Dottie and me. I need a distraction."

"I plan to do more than distract you, Anna." His cocky grin made her step out of the circle of his arms as heat raced into her face. "Come on."

He led her though the crowd. An easy silence fell between them as they walked among the tents that dotted the field. The smell of charcoal drifted on the breeze. Enough watermelons to fill a field loaded one table. Men in uniform walked with women dressed in Sunday dresses. Everyone had worn their best to honor the country's birthday.

"Different footraces are taking place to the west of the field." Sid turned in that direction. "And over there"—he pointed east—"is where the fireworks will shoot off at dusk. They shipped them in from New York, so it should be a great display."

The hours flew by. First, they munched on juicy burgers and slices of sweet watermelon. Then Sid tried to talk her into a three-legged race.

"Come on. We could beat everyone here."

Anna eyed the couples assembled and grimaced. "I've never been athletic."

"That doesn't matter. It's a field race. How hard can it be?"

Five minutes later, Anna laughed until she felt breathless. "This is why I'm not athletic."

"Naw. I'd call it uncoordinated." Sid collapsed next to her and untied the strips of cloth binding them together.

Anna stuck out her tongue at him. "I'm not sure that's much better. Besides, what do you expect when I'm handicapped by this skirt?"

"Let's head over to the parade field and get a good seat for the fireworks."

"Isn't it early?"

"Never too early to sit down with a beautiful woman and get to know her better."

Anna let his words wash over her as he turned to telling her stories about his early days in the army—story after story about basic training and the shenanigans he and the other drafted men had pulled.

"So how many of these pranks did you instigate?"

Sid shrugged, color rising in his cheeks. "One or two. Somebody had to create ways to keep the new guys on their toes."

"And how often did you get KP duty?"

"Not often enough. I kept coming up with new ways to get the fresh recruits involved."

"What was your favorite?"

"Favorite joke? I don't know. I've left those days behind me. Now I'm an upstanding citizen who never does anything crazy."

Anna rolled her eyes. "I'm supposed to believe that?" A glint filled Sid's eyes, and Anna wondered if she'd pushed too far. "On second thought, don't answer that question. I'm sure you've outgrown fun."

"I guess I'll have to prove it to you."

Before she could respond, the initial flurry of fireworks launched. The explosions filled the sky with color and the field with waves of smoke. When the display ended, Sid walked her to the bus.

"Will I see you this weekend?" Sid held on to her hand, his fingers laced through hers as she stood at the base of the bus's stairs.

"Only if you bring prisoners to help with the detasseling." She sighed. The work was hot and miserable no matter how you looked at it. The wheat was barely in, and now the corn demanded attention. "If I were you, I'd take an assignment that moves you anywhere but toward our farm."

Sid leaned in closer, and Anna found it hard to breathe. "I'll be there with plenty of help. Haven't you figured out that I care about you?"

seventeen

Long days filled the rest of Anna's week as she made up the extra time off on the Fourth. By Friday, all Anna wanted to do was crawl into bed for the weekend. Instead, the weekend at home would be filled with physical labor far beyond the normal effort of cleaning the house and catching up on chores.

Detasseling corn was an essential yet dreaded part of summer. Every year it arrived like clockwork. Every year it threatened to sap every last ounce of her energy. She'd felt that way even in years when she didn't work in a factory more than forty hours a week.

This year she couldn't imagine where she'd find the strength to endure the grueling labor.

As Dottie prepared to turn into Anna's driveway, Anna longed to tell her to keep driving. She'd spend the weekend at her friend's house instead. Dottie wouldn't mind. However, much as Anna loved her roommate, she looked forward to closing the door at the end of a long day and being alone. That happened far too infrequently.

"Do you want me to come back tomorrow and help?"

Anna grimaced at the thought. Dottie had never worked that hard in her life. "You've put your time in. Go home and relax. Do that for me, too."

"I'd come."

"I appreciate it. No reason for both of us to be covered in cuts and blisters on Monday."

Dottie's eyes danced even as she plastered a frown on her face. "Fine, keep all the fun to yourself. See you Sunday night. I'll come around six."

Anna climbed out of the car and waved good-bye. Then she trudged toward the house.

❧

Saturday morning, Papa pounded on Anna's bedroom door while it was still dark.

Anna stretched. "I'll be there in a minute." She stifled a yawn and walked to the window. Pushing back the curtain, she saw the first hints of dawn painting the sky. Heaviness cloaked her at the thought of the day. *Father, help me survive this day. And help me find a way to serve You in the midst of it.*

Anna slipped outside at five thirty and stopped to appreciate the sun cresting the horizon. Colors glowed across its lower sweeps. While such sights used to be routine, it had been months since she'd risen this early. She shivered in the chill air. Tires crunched against the gravel driveway. She turned to see two trucks entering the farmyard. One bore the marks and coloring of a military truck. The other looked like Gus's old beater. Her heart jumped at the sight of Sid climbing out of the first truck.

Half a dozen prisoners climbed from the back of the truck, clad in their jeans and denim shirts. They didn't carry any sort of jackets, which they'd need in the early morning hours until the sun burned the dew off the corn. Then they'd swelter the rest of the day under the glaring sun without any covering to shield them.

Gus, Teddy, and a few of the older men from church climbed out of Gus's truck. They'd come prepared with rain slickers. They eyed the prisoners then ambled to the back door to join Papa. He looked wide awake and ready to tackle the task. Something hard but resigned entered his face when he looked at the Germans.

"Who's going to teach them?" He thrust his chin in their direction.

Anna shrugged. "You."

"I haven't taught them a thing."

That explained the undirected activities she'd seen them engaged in on other trips to the farm. "Someone has to make sure they know what they're doing." Papa crossed his arms and stared at her. The other men refused to meet her eyes. She rubbed her face and groaned. "Fine. I'll take care of that." She turned and headed into the house.

"Where are you going, girl?"

"If these men are headed into the fields, they're going to need some bandannas. Don't worry—I'll let them use mine, Papa."

In a minute she came back out, loaded down with bandannas and hats. She thrust them at Sid. "Make sure they wear these. You don't want them to get corn rash if we can help it."

"Corn rash?" Sid looked at her with a blank expression.

"Trust me. It's bad." Anna returned to Papa. "Which field do you want them in?"

"We'll take the middle field. They can work the south field. And don't forget we'll need a big lunch."

Anna rolled her eyes. Of course they would. "I'll see what I can pull together while teaching these men what to do." Before she said something she shouldn't, she turned and headed toward the field. After a moment, she swiveled and put her hands on her hips. "Are you coming?"

Sid stared at her. "Coming where?"

"Time to get these men to work." She took off again, satisfied when she heard the sound of footsteps behind her. When she reached the edge of the field, she turned and waited for the others to catch up. "Tell them to sit down. It'll take a minute to explain what they need to do."

Once the men crouched on the ground, Anna took a bandanna and hat from Sid. She put them on, the bandanna tied securely around her neck. "Tell them to do the same."

He pantomimed what she had done, and Anna tried not to laugh. "Know much German?"

"Nope. They do know some English. Franz here"—he gestured at a rail-thin blond man—"does a decent job interpreting if you keep the words simple."

"All right." Anna walked toward the field. "You'll each take a row. Pull the plant down; remove the tassels off the top."

She pulled down a plant and grimaced as dew sprayed her face. "You'll repeat to the end of the row. Then start again. We've got one hundred some acres of corn, so it'll take a couple of days if we're lucky."

Sid watched her motions as she demonstrated detasseling on a few more plants. "Are you staying out here with us?"

"For a while."

"Doesn't look like you're tall enough to do this."

She stared at him, mouth agape. Was that a challenge? Sure sounded like one. "I've detasseled corn for years. Where there's a will, there's a way."

He looked her up and down, and she stood tall on her toes. A twinkle filled his eyes. "All right, sprite, let's see who reaches the end of a row quickest."

It really wasn't a fair contest. Her experience would beat his height any day. She pulled her gloves from the back of her waistband. "Fine. Let's go. You take that row, and I'll grab this one. Get the prisoners started, and then we're on."

He eyed her gloves. "Have any more of those?"

"Sorry. You should have brought your own." It wouldn't be a fair fight if he didn't have them. His hands wouldn't last twenty plants without protection. "Did any of you bring gloves?"

Sid glanced at the truck then shrugged. "Don't think so."

The prisoner named Luka raised his hand. "We bring gloves."

"Let me borrow a pair."

"Sure thing, boss."

"Guess you're here to supervise." Anna smirked at him. In a minute all the prisoners but Luka were in their rows and pulling tassels from the corn. "Showtime. Take your row."

Sid tugged the gloves on and took a ready stance.

"Go."

Anna entered the row. It felt like she'd stepped into a shower. In moments, the dew drenched her, and her shoes stuck in the mud. Her arms and shoulders ached as she switched from side to side, grabbing tassels on the plants. Some plants were her height; for others she had to stretch as far as she could to reach the tops.

Her legs throbbed from plodding through the mud as she marched methodically down the row. Amid the rustling of cornstalks and leaves, she heard an occasional grunt from Sid. He really shouldn't have laid down the challenge. She'd lived on a farm her entire life, and until he'd reached Camp Atlanta, he'd never stepped foot on one. Poor city boy.

There. She could finally see the end of the row. How were Papa and his gang going to hold up? They were too old for this. This was a young person's job. Her neck twinged. A much younger person. If the soldiers couldn't work, maybe she'd hire kids from church.

She pushed through the last plants and stopped.

Sid lay on the ground, arms spread, chest heaving. "Looks like I won."

"Humph. I think I'll check your row on the way back."

He waggled his eyebrows at her, and she couldn't help laughing. "So your height is an advantage."

"Maybe."

"I'll walk your row, and then you need to make sure all the prisoners are doing a good job. If one plant is missed, it can ruin the whole crop."

"Why?"

"It's a hybrid crop, and detasseling's the only way to keep it that way. I'll stick around for a bit; then I have to make lunch."

The morning passed quickly with the prisoners working steadily across the rows. As she checked their work, she found they'd done a thorough job and needed only minimal redirection and cleanup. Maybe this would work.

She hurried back to the house and stoked the fire on the stove. Biscuits and gravy with applesauce and green beans would have to do the trick. It was all she could find to fill the quantities needed. She finished the meal then rang the bell on the side of the house. The men and prisoners trickled into the yard.

Gus limped to a stop next to the door. "Can I help with anything, Miss Anna?"

"Please rest. I've got everything ready."

Teddy and the other men from church didn't look much better than Gus. Teddy kept a hand anchored to his back, then sank to the ground with a sigh. Only Papa looked like he had any energy for the afternoon. *Probably because he hasn't done anything for months.*

She served them at a table she'd pulled into the yard. The men dug into the bowls of food and filled glasses with water and milk. Anna hoped enough would remain for the prisoners. The prisoners and Sid walked into the yard. While quiet, they looked ready for more work that afternoon. Anna pulled out some blankets and handed them to Sid.

"These can go on the ground." She collected extra bowls from inside and placed them in the center of the blankets. She tried to ignore the storm cloud gathering on Papa's brow. "Here. Have the men sit down and eat. They've earned it."

Sid stepped in front of her. "Anna, the prisoners aren't supposed to eat with you."

"Why on earth not? They worked as hard as everyone else."

"It's against regulations."

"Yet another reason not to have them here. If I can't provide for them like other hired help, then you can keep them at Atlanta." The murmured sound of German filtered toward her. She stood with arms crossed staring Sid down.

Sid hesitated then waved the prisoners forward. The prisoners collapsed on the blankets and filled plates with food.

Papa stood with a roar. "Get these men off my lawn. Ain't it bad enough what they've done to my boy? You insist on feeding them, too?"

Anna's mouth fell open. She tried to speak but couldn't find her voice.

Papa spun and disappeared inside the house. A moment later, the screen door slammed against the side of the house, and Papa barreled out with a shotgun. "Get them away."

"Papa. You don't mean that."

The prisoners stopped eating and stared at the gun.

"Get them off now."

"How will we finish without their help?"

"I don't need Krauts to do that." The shotgun quivered in Papa's grip.

Gus stood and approached his friend. "It's okay."

"No, it ain't. Nothing about this situation is right."

"Let's go inside." Gus forced Papa to join him inside.

Anna stared after them, unsure what to do next.

"Maybe I should pack them up and leave." Sid joined her, standing shoulder to shoulder with her.

"Maybe." But if he did, how would she get all the detasseling done? Her muscles quaked from the few rows and cleanup she'd done. That was nothing compared to doing row after row. She turned so Sid couldn't see her chin quiver. She would not cry in front of him. She couldn't. Once she started, she didn't know if she'd ever stop.

eighteen

Sid stared at Anna, wanting to take her in his arms but unconvinced she wanted that. Instead, he stood with his arms hanging at his sides, his feet shifting awkwardly as he watched her fight for control. Would she ever realize she could depend on him? That he didn't see her as a burden? That he wanted—no, longed—to help?

After a minute, he cleared his throat. "Will you finish the detasseling without help?"

She shook her head. She stood a moment longer then sucked in a deep breath. "Don't worry about us. I'll get us through this."

"Maybe you don't have to."

She whirled on him, eyes blazing, though extra bright. "What? Have a plan up your sleeve to keep the prisoners here without Papa shooting them? I've carried this place for more than a year. I'll keep doing it."

"All I'm saying is you don't have to do it alone. We can keep your dad away from the prisoners. Keep the reminder out of sight." Sid pulled off his hat then raked his fingers through his hair.

"You think I can't handle this." The set of her chin matched the tone of her words.

How was he supposed to respond to that? No, he didn't think a woman could handle a farm of more than three hundred acres on her own. Especially when she worked four to five days a week in a factory. He didn't know many men who could do that. Somehow he sensed she wouldn't accept that.

"Look, you don't have to do anything to convince me you're an incredible person. But everybody needs help." He glanced at the prisoners.

The six men had finished their lunch. Several now lay on the blankets. Luka eyed him, a stiff air about him as if he understood the tension that crackled in the air. Luka gestured to the men. Time to get back to work?

Sid nodded. He'd get the men back into the field. Too much work remained to waste time talking about things he couldn't fix. Anna's father wouldn't change unless he wanted to. That didn't alter the fact that acres of corn remained to be detasseled.

"We'll be in the field if you need us." He went to where his men stood before Anna could protest. She might not like his methods, but better to start before her father returned and tore into a German.

By the end of the day, Sid gladly hauled himself into the truck. With a few groans and mild complaints, the prisoners collapsed in its bed. Once they'd settled, Sid headed back to Camp Atlanta. It had been a long day. Since lunch, Anna had avoided him as if he had a contagious disease, but she also hadn't ordered them to leave.

Already his shoulders and back ached from the work. He had a feeling by morning he'd feel all kinds of other muscles he'd forgotten. Anyone who thought farmers had an easy life hadn't spent a day like his.

Problem was that after a full fourteen hours in the fields, they'd barely covered a third of the corn. Sure, by the end of the day, the men were more proficient at the work. But it had taken too long to reach that point. Tomorrow had to go faster. He'd attend the early chapel service then head back. Luka promised he'd have the men ready.

The old men had creaked through their rows. Sid supposed their help was better than nothing, but they needed more hands. He'd bring more prisoners tomorrow, except he needed approval. The prisoners were spread thin between the local farmers and branch camps. With the fields planted and crops growing, work wasn't in short supply. No, the farmers needed and valued the prisoners' labor. Even folks who felt like Anna's dad. Fortunately, Mr. Goodman hadn't come back out after Gus led him inside.

As soon as he reached his barracks, Sid dropped onto his bed and kicked off his boots. In minutes, he fell asleep.

Sunday passed in a blur of repetitive motion. Anna remained aloof until Sid decided she'd pouted long enough.

As the prisoners marched to the truck, he stalked up to her. "Be ready in an hour."

"For what?" She crossed her arms and stared at him.

"I'm coming back and getting you away from here. We've worked hard, and it's time to relax."

"But Dottie will be here soon."

"When?"

"Around six."

Sid frowned. "Tell her to wait. I'll bring something back for all of us." He squared his jaw. She couldn't put him off that easily. "Don't go anywhere until I get back."

He turned toward the truck but could swear he caught her sticking out her tongue in his peripheral vision. If he weren't so tired, he'd smile. Crazy girl had spunk.

After returning the prisoners to their compound, Sid flew through a shower and into clean clothes. He pulled out of Camp Atlanta and drove to Atlanta. He reached the little café in town thirty minutes before it closed and grabbed a quick picnic of fried chicken and potato salad.

When he pulled into the Goodmans' lane, Dottie's car stood next to the house. He released a breath at the realization that Anna had waited. Maybe she wasn't as angry with him as she acted. He hopped out of his car and hurried toward the house.

"We're over here."

He found the girls lounging in chairs next to the barn. Anna looked wrung out, her face pink with sunburn, short curls tucked behind her ears. Her eyes were closed, a tired smile on her lips. Even exhausted, she took his breath away. He tried to rein in his thoughts. The important thing was discussing how she'd make it through a week in Kearney after the weekend she'd had. And how the detasseling would be finished while she did.

Dottie smiled at him, a hint of Mary Martin flashing in her grin. "I'd begun to think Anna lied about you coming back." She looked over his shoulder. "Bring anyone with you?"

Sid shook his head and shrugged. Hadn't crossed his mind, even if he'd had time to grab someone like Trent.

"I'll entertain myself while you guys enjoy your dinner."

"There's plenty here."

"Thanks, but I don't like playing third wheel." She stood and slapped Anna lightly on the cheek. Anna opened her eyes and glanced up at her. "We leave in forty-five minutes."

"Sure you don't want to eat with us?"

"Certain. I'll be over by the apple trees."

Sid watched Dottie head off. Why hadn't he thought to bring Trent with him? Anna shifted in her chair, and he pulled his attention back to important matters. "I brought some chicken."

"Thank you."

Sid pulled out the meat, salad, plates, and silverware. Once they each had a plate, he said a quick grace. Silence settled between them as they ate. When he'd cleared his plate, he set it aside and focused on Anna.

"I'll bring the prisoners back until the job is done. Hopefully we'll finish before Jude reassigns them."

"He's never liked Papa much."

Sid could imagine. If the man had always been this prickly, it was easy to understand. But Gus and Teddy seemed to genuinely like him, so something at the core of the man had appealed to others at one time.

"Maybe Papa's right." Anna's sigh resonated with heaviness. "Maybe I need to quit at the air base and stay here for a while. There's no way he can handle the farm. Yesterday made that clear if I didn't already know it."

"Do you like your job?"

"It's fine, and I'm making a difference. The boys need those parachutes packed properly. I've gotten good at it." She set her plate on the ground. "The problem is, if I come home, I don't know how I'll stand it."

"Do you like the farm?"

"Doesn't matter."

"Yes, it does. You seem to come back week after week because you feel a sense of duty. But I haven't seen you enjoy it."

Fire sparked in her eyes. "What about my life am I supposed to love right now? I have a father who is angry. All the time. I have a job that requires long hours. I live in a small room in a boardinghouse with my best friend. I come home on weekends and work until I'm past exhausted. What part should I enjoy?"

"The fact you're alive. That you live in a free country. Maybe the fact that God loves you. That He's given you a job to do whether it's in Kearney or here." Sid stopped, counted to ten. Where had this rush of words erupted from? "When I look at you, I see a beautiful woman who has a lot to offer, but you're held back by cares you carry alone."

Anna stared openmouthed at him, color flashing up her face.

Sid raked a hand through his hair. How could he explain what he saw in a way that she would accept? "Frankly, I think you're needed here this week. There's a lot that must happen to maintain the crops. You said yourself if the detasseling isn't done, it could ruin the entire crop of corn. But if you don't want to stay, go.

"Whatever you choose, you need to decide in your heart that you're going to find a way to release the load. You can't carry everyone else's burdens for them."

Her mouth opened and shut like that of a trout pulled out of a stream, desperate for water. She snapped her lips together and hurried after Dottie.

Sid's shoulders sagged as she got into the car without a word to him. Guess she'd made her decision about what to do. He watched her go and wondered if his words had ended any hope of more than a tentative friendship with her.

He turned toward the fields. The corn waved in rows across the land, seemingly unending.

If he wanted to bring more prisoners to work tomorrow, he needed to return to camp. He'd bring as many men as he could. Get the job done and move on. Anna had made it clear that she didn't want his help or his friendship. And her father didn't hide his feelings.

Turning to his car, Sid caught Mr. Goodman watching him through the kitchen window. Sid waved at the man—sooner or later he had to soften. And maybe his daughter would join him.

nineteen

"Anna Goodman, I have had enough. It is time to stop moping." Dottie plopped down on the bed across from Anna's, a mock frown plastered on her face. "Get dressed in your prettiest skirt and blouse. We're going to the USO tonight."

Anna stared at Dottie, mouth hanging open.

"What? Aren't you tired of sitting here long in the face? I know I'm sick of watching you. Time to get your focus off yourself and onto somebody else. Who, I don't care. Anybody will do." Dottie launched off the bed and scurried to the wardrobe. She pulled a skirt off its hanger and threw it at Anna. "Here. Put this one on."

"I'll pick out my clothes. First, you have to tell me where you think you're taking me."

"The USO. Didn't you listen to me?" Dottie heaved a dramatic sigh. She playfully pushed Anna to her feet. "Come on. You'll have fun. Might even meet some nice people and get a life beyond me."

A very unladylike snort escaped before Anna could stifle it. "I doubt that. Then you would need another life to run." Dottie's eyes sparkled, and she tapped her toes. Anna might as well give in to the inevitable. "Give me fifteen minutes, and I'll be ready."

"With bells on your toes."

"Yes, ma'am." A melody hummed out of Anna. It would do her good to forget about everything for a bit. She pulled out a dress with a bodice that crossed in front with a beautiful drape. The large-flowered print always brought a smile to her face. She slipped into the dress then put on a pair of baby doll heels. She added a veiled beret to her curls and adjusted it while looking in the mirror. She already felt better, more positive about the evening. It had been too long since she'd dressed up like this.

"Ready?"

"Just a minute." Anna grabbed an eyebrow pencil and ran it up the back of each leg. She twisted but couldn't tell if she'd gotten them right. "Do those look straight?"

Dottie eyed the lines then nodded. "Let's scoot. The guys'll be here soon to pick us up."

Anna stopped and stared at Dottie. "I didn't sign up to go with somebody. I'm not in the mood for a date."

"It's not like that. One of the soldiers is a pal of mine. He's grabbed a buddy, and they'll escort us. We won't be tied down to one person, and neither will they."

Sure. That's what she'd said the last time she got them into a situation like this. Anna plopped down on the bed and removed the pins from her hat. "I'm not interested."

"You don't have to be. Didn't you hear a thing I said? Some days it feels like your ears don't work." Dottie flopped down next to her. "They're our ride. I'm not made of gasoline rations, you know. But it's important to get you out. I suppose we could ask another boarder to go with us and drive."

Anna shuddered. The other gals were nice enough, she supposed, but Anna hadn't made the time to get to know them beyond the basics. Sometimes she wondered what had happened to her. She used to love getting to know new people. Now she didn't have the energy.

The doorbell's ring echoed up the stairs.

Dottie stood and thrust her hands on her hips. "You can stay here and mope all you like. I'm going out tonight. If I can encourage a few soldiers, I'll consider the night a success." She grabbed her flap bag and left the small room.

The walls closed in on Anna as Dottie clunked down the stairs. She needed to go. She'd already dressed for the evening. No need to waste that effort.

"Wait, Dottie. I'm coming." Anna placed her hat back on her head and flew down the stairs. Two soldiers dressed in their dress uniforms waited inside the door.

"Anna, I'd like you to meet my friend John Chester and his friend Thomas Reynolds. Gents, let's hit the road." Dottie linked arms with John, leaving Thomas staring at Anna through narrowed eyes. She tried not to squirm under his intense scrutiny.

Anna nodded toward the door. "Shall we join them?"

He tipped his head. "After you."

The USO hummed with music and the conversation of at least one hundred people. The air stifled Anna. Add all the bodies to the residual heat, and the room seemed very closed. Thomas tried to lead her to the dance floor, but she resisted.

"I'm not ready to dance yet. Why don't we sit down and chat for a while?"

He answered each question with a monosyllable. His eyes darted around the room until she looked over her shoulder to follow his glance. She grinned at the realization that he was watching the girls at the food tables. Color climbed his neck when he caught her. He stood abruptly. "Can I get you something to drink?"

"That would be great." She watched him walk away. This exchange reflected why she hated coming to these events. Stilted conversations with people she didn't know and didn't care to know. Some people had the gift of gab, but she didn't. Didn't think she wanted it, either. Why couldn't more men be like Sid Chance?

She stilled.

Where had that thought come from? Many of their inter-actions ended in near arguments.

"May I have this dance?"

Anna looked up into eyes that were so deeply blue they almost matched the sunset but were filled with a twinkle that had nothing to do with stars. He smiled as he held out his hand.

"Private Trent Franklin at your service."

Anna stood and accepted his hand. He eased her onto the

dance floor as Bing Crosby crooned some tune. It sounded like "White Christmas," which didn't make much sense in the middle of July.

Private Franklin was a quiet man, but Anna didn't mind. She closed her eyes and enjoyed the moment. Before she knew it, the dance with him led to others with different soldiers. Most wanted to dance, and those who talked didn't expect her to do anything other than listen. That she could do.

"Anna."

She turned from the circle of Private Franklin's arms to find Dottie waving for her from near the door.

"We have to leave."

"Thank you for an enjoyable evening, Private."

"My pleasure. I don't think I caught your name, though."

"Now that seems odd. We've spent several dances together."

"If you leave now, I'll have to call you my mystery lady."

Anna smiled. "I like the sound of that. Good night." She slipped away before he could say anything else.

The next morning, her duties at the air base seemed less tedious. New energy had infused her. Dottie had been right. She needed to get out and forget about herself for a while, focus on others and on making them smile. It hadn't been too hard once she got into the swing of it.

She caressed the silk parachute she held. Would this parachute save a soldier's life someday? Maybe somebody like her brother? Then all the struggles, the exhaustion, would be worth it.

❧

By Friday morning, Sid had decided farming wasn't the life for him. He'd had it after a week of taking the prisoners around the Goodman acres, stripping the corn of its tassels, and weeding after that. The only good news was they'd finish today. The other field at the far end of the farm contained regular corn rather than seed corn, so those plants kept their tassels. Today he felt grateful for the small things.

Trent Franklin walked back from getting the last prisoner

settled in his row. "Looks like you're all done in."

"Feels that way." Sid leaned against the truck and closed his eyes. The sun beat down on him.

"You should have come with me last night."

"After working like a dog all week? Franklin, I don't know where you get the energy, but I'm glad I fell into bed."

Trent leaned against the truck next to him and stuck a stalk of wheat between his teeth. "There was this girl I danced with. You would have liked her, though I'm glad you weren't there to compete with me. I'll never understand why gals flock to you when I'm standing right here with my good looks."

"If you like Danny Kaye."

"Exactly. Lean, lanky, that's me." Trent pulled the stalk from his mouth and struck a pose. "Not tall and rugged like you. Anyway, this gal was a looker. Short blond curls. Perky little nose. Come to think of it, she looked a lot like Miss Goodman. And she wouldn't tell me her name. What do you think of that?"

"Sounds like she wanted to play and not get involved."

"See, that's what I'm thinking." He shrugged. "You know, I think she could serve as Anna's twin. Even sounded like her. Not giving me her name. She thought I already knew it."

Sid fought the heat that enveloped his gut. He'd spent the week slaving in her fields. And she danced the night away? He couldn't decide whether to be angry with her or concerned that she'd loosened up.

Trent pushed off the truck. "I'll go walk the rows a bit. Check on the prisoners. You stay here and rest. You need it."

Sure he did. All because he worked hard for a gal who didn't notice or care. Well, he was finished being her lackey. He'd find someone who appreciated him without letting him work to the bone.

Even as the thoughts assaulted him, he wondered if he could be happy with anybody else.

twenty

The door to Commander Moss's office stood open, and Sid spied him sitting behind his desk, working on paperwork. If that was how officers spent their time, Sid would stay at his current rank. He'd rather invest in people. He rapped on the doorframe.

Commander Moss looked up. "Come in, soldier."

"Specialist Chance reporting, sir." Sid stood at attention in front of the desk.

"At ease, Specialist." Commander Moss shifted some papers on his desk until he found what he wanted. "I've got orders sending you to the Grand Island satellite for a week. We've got a group of prisoners who need transport. You'll oversee that, then report back on the camp's status. I hear rumors of trouble and want it taken care of now."

Sid reached for the paperwork and swallowed. If he could pick, he didn't want to leave. He and Anna had some issues to work through. Unfortunately, the army didn't care about such personal issues. "When do we leave?"

"Tomorrow morning. The prisoners report to work Monday. Take enough time to evaluate the situation. I need eyes and ears on the ground."

"Yes, sir."

"That's all." Commander Moss turned back to his work.

Sid snapped a salute then spun and exited the room. There went his plans for the weekend. At least he wouldn't spend the next few days surrounded by corn. His skin itched at the thought. He'd never been so glad to finish a task in his life.

The only problem came from missing Anna. He'd planned to spend time with her while on his A pass. He'd earned that much. Guess he'd pocket the pass for another time. Maybe he'd find someone to spend time with at the Grand Island USO. The idea didn't excite him like he'd expected. There'd been many a day when the mere thought of spending time with a pretty gal would bring a lift to his mood. Today that didn't happen. Anna had crept further into his mind and heart than he'd realized.

Maybe he should take the time to pray about what to do with Anna. She remained a complete puzzle to him. A frustrating one, but one he couldn't shake.

❧

Anna watched Dottie throw a couple of blouses into her bag. For once, Anna would stay in Kearney for the weekend. The thought of spending the days right here, in her room, sounded wonderful.

"Sure you don't want to come see a certain soldier?"

"There's no guarantee he'll come to the farm."

Dottie snorted. "Sure. And cows are purple."

"He didn't seem very happy with me last weekend. Based on that, I'd be surprised if he came around while I'm there." Anna fluffed up her pillow then leaned against it. "I need some time alone. Time to think and pray. Figure out where I'm supposed to focus my energy and attention."

"You mean you've finally heard everything I've said?" Dottie zipped up her bag and plopped next to Anna. "If that's what you're going to do, stay. Just make sure you don't have fun without me."

"Yes, Mom."

"Maybe I should stay and supervise."

Anna shook her head. "No, I need solitude. At least as much as I can get in a boardinghouse. Maybe if I slow down awhile, I'll hear something."

"You don't need me for that." Dottie hopped up and grabbed her bag. "Ta-ta. See you on Sunday."

The door closed behind Dottie, and Anna sank onto the bed. If she let herself, she could sleep the entire weekend. While that might feel wonderful, she really needed time to think. Maybe she felt so out of sorts in recent weeks because she hadn't taken time to care for herself. The very idea seemed odd, but the more she'd prayed this week, the more she'd sensed the need—at the core of her being —to stop for a couple of days and reconnect with her heavenly Father.

Anna startled awake. Long shadows filled the room, and her stomach growled. She glanced at the clock. Eight o'clock. Too late to ask Mrs. Wisdom for supper. Anna grabbed her clutch and hat and headed outside. She'd walk the couple of blocks to the café, see if they still served supper. Skipping meals hadn't been part of her plan.

She strolled into the café, a hole-in-the-wall tucked between a shoe store and a small grocer. Couples sat at two of the tables, and a waitress stood at a counter, smacking gum while reading a copy of *Life*. Anna took a seat at the counter.

"Can I help you?" The waitress didn't look up from her magazine.

"Are you serving dinner?"

"Not anymore. Pie or coffee?"

Two slices of pie rested in the display case. "I guess I'll have the apple."

"Pear?"

"Fine. With a cup of coffee, please."

The waitress slapped the pie on a plate and slid it with a cup of coffee to Anna. "Enjoy."

This hadn't been how she envisioned starting her free weekend. As the piecrust melted on her tongue, she decided it wasn't a half-bad way, after all. She paid and then headed back outside. The night felt mild, with a breeze to ease the earlier heat.

Images of Papa filled her mind. Without a phone at the house, she couldn't tell him she wouldn't be coming home. By now, he'd probably figured that out, if he even missed her.

She savored the freedom Kearney offered. Papa couldn't yell that she was terrible or lazy. He would never understand how it felt to listen to his words day after day. But his silence was worse, leaving her guessing what she'd done wrong.

The thought of spending more time at home with him made her want to curl into a corner and hide. Yet the more she prayed, the more that seemed the only solution.

Saturday, Anna spent the morning in her room, reading her Bible and praying. By noon, beads of sweat rolled down her cheeks. Her mind wandered as the blanket of heat weighed down on her. No matter how hard she tried to quiet her thoughts, they refused to cooperate.

Instead, her ears seemed tuned to the sounds of the building. As the morning passed, her heart sank that Sid hadn't called for her.

"Enough." Anna threw her Bible next to her on the bed. "Time to do something."

Maybe if she walked around a bit, she could regain her focus. Work off the malaise that sapped her energy. She pulled on her loafers and headed for the stairs.

"Anna, you're in time." Betsy Turner clapped her hands together. "I wanted to knock on your door, but you were so quiet I was afraid I'd wake you."

Anna snorted. As if she'd ever slept to noon in her life. Showed how little Betsy knew her. "What did you need?"

Betsy turned to the soldiers with her. "We were headed to the USO for a while. There's a lunch and afternoon activities there today. Join us? We need a fourth," she implored with eyes wide.

The two soldiers stood at ease, looking everywhere but at her. She'd seen the shorter one with Betsy before. But the taller, lanky one was new. It couldn't hurt anything to spend time with them. Anna wondered briefly about returning to her room, but after a morning locked in there, she couldn't stomach the thought.

"All right. Let me grab my bag." She scooted upstairs long enough to get her purse and touch up her lipstick.

Betsy introduced her to the two soldiers, and they headed to the USO. Anna's escort, Sammy Kersh, sat next to her in the car. When they arrived, the USO burst at the seams with soldiers and local girls. Anna wondered if she'd ever see it any way but packed. How could she feel so alone when surrounded by so many people? She caught the eyes of several soldiers watching her, but each took one look at her escort and turned around.

"Do you mind?"

Sammy locked his deep brown eyes on her and grinned. "Mind?"

"I'm feeling a bit cornered." Anna crossed her arms and met his gaze with a glare.

"I don't know why."

"You're stuck to me like a burr to a steer."

Sam threw back his head and laughed. Anna bit the inside of her lip to hide the smile that wanted to escape.

"How about I do something about that?"

Anna held her tongue and hardened her expression while she waited for him to elaborate.

Sam held up his hands. "Listen, the band's started. Let's take a whirl around the floor. Then we'll grab a plate of food and head outside where we can find a quiet place to talk."

He tugged her after him onto the floor. He led her through the steps with self-assurance. Anna tried to focus on him and the moment, but Sid's clear blue eyes kept invading her thoughts.

"What brings you to Kearney?"

"What brings anyone?" Sam shrugged. "My crew is collecting our B-17. We'll ship out in a week or as soon as we've completed all the flight checks."

The song ended, and he led her to the tables loaded with sandwiches and salads. The conversation continued while they filled their plates. In a few moments, they settled in the shade of a large oak tree. It stood in a secluded location behind the building. Anna looked around, surprised to find that no other couples had ventured outside away from the closed air of the hall.

Sam settled on the ground and edged closer until their legs touched. She pulled her legs beneath her and eased some space between them. Sam eyed her over his meal, almost as if he wanted her for dessert. She tried to swallow a bite of her chicken sandwich, but it tasted like sandpaper.

"Come here, Anna."

"I think we're quite close enough." If he got any closer, she'd leave. Coming to the USO looked like an increasingly bad decision with each minute.

Sam edged toward her. "Never close enough."

"You are no gentleman."

His eyes laughed at her. "I never said I was."

"I'm not interested in being any closer." Anna stood and pushed her plate of food in his lap. "You can find someone else to spend the rest of your afternoon with."

She shook and felt sick to her stomach as she headed to the street. Betsy could catch up with her at the Wisdoms'. Thank goodness, the walk wouldn't take all day.

As the blocks passed, her heart returned to its normal patterns. One thought cycled through her mind. In all her interactions with Sid, he had never once treated her with anything less than complete respect. She rubbed her arms, trying to bring some warmth, wishing Sid were here.

twenty-one

Grand Island, though larger than Holdrege or Kearney, didn't fit the bill for Sid that weekend. Even when the other soldiers headed out to explore the local scene, Sid stayed behind. Then he'd wanted to check his temperature, see what was wrong. By Monday, he couldn't wait to get to work, discover what concerned Commander Moss, and return to Camp Atlanta.

Anything would be better than spending every waking moment wondering what one young woman was doing. He hated the fact that Anna Goodman had crept under his guard.

His style was to enjoy whatever woman he found himself matched with. Now he mooned over a girl who drove him batty. A gal who forever surprised him. And a woman who made him want to drop everything and protect her.

What magic had she worked on him?

Monday morning, Sid strode into the satellite headquarters and introduced himself to the officer in charge. He tried to cover his surprise when he learned that Larry Heglin filled that bill.

"Commander Moss asked me to spend some time with you this week and see how we could better support your operations in Grand Island."

Heglin sneered at him from behind his desk. "We're just fine, Chance. I've got things humming along without any interference from the bigwigs." He kicked back and stared down his nose at Sid. "Why would Moss send someone like you here, anyway? You're the one who lost the prisoner. Still trying to get in his good graces?"

Sid stiffened his back. Heat climbed his neck, and he tried to force it back with a deep breath. "I'll spend the day with the prisoners at their assignment. Check their quarters tonight."

"Waste your time all you want. I don't know what you think you'll find. The prisoners are fine, the employers pleased. That's all the army can want."

Sid strode from the room. Of all the people who could command the post, he had to deal with someone as incompetent as Heglin. Yet another reason to get in and get out. It would have helped if Commander Moss had told him anything about why he was here. He hadn't picked up anything over the weekend. But most of the soldiers were on passes with just a couple left to guard the prisoners.

He strode around the compound. The army had retrofitted the old Dodge School to meet its needs. An eight-foot fence towered around the school with a couple of men and dogs patrolling the perimeter. Directly across the street stood the German American social club at Liederkranz Hall. Polka music had blasted from the facility over the weekend, but nothing that concerned Sid.

A bus stood outside the front door, and a steady line of prisoners boarded it. They stood with heads high, and quiet conversation flowed among them. From all outward appearances, they seemed content—at least as much as they could for people thousands of miles from home.

Sid made a mental note to learn who served as prisoner liaison and spend time with him. Until then, he'd circulate among them, see what he could pick up. He hadn't heard of aggressive Nazis being relocated from this group, so he didn't expect that to be the challenge.

The bus rumbled over the road until it reached the beet fields where the prisoners worked. The day passed with Sid talking to the prisoners or their guards and finding each group equally unwilling to cooperate.

At this rate, he'd have to spend a year here to learn anything.

Sid kicked back on his bunk that night, trying to stay as quiet as possible as the soldiers bantered around him. Maybe they'd forget he was there.

"Did you see what Heglin did today?" A skinny soldier with a Bronx accent spoke from the doorway.

A soldier lying back on his bed snorted. "You mean he actually left his desk? That guy likes to sit and look important rather than do anything."

"Sure, but today he strolled around surveying his kingdom after you left. I thought he acted kind of funny, so I kept an eye on him. He headed into the prisoner section. When he came out, he had a funny look on his face and loaded pockets."

"So? What's the big deal with that?"

"I don't know. Thought it interesting since he avoids the Germans like they've got some kind'a disease." He pushed away from the door. "I'll never understand why someone like him was put in charge."

"That's the army for ya. Always makes perfect sense."

The men chortled then wandered into topics that held no interest for Sid. He couldn't imagine what Heglin could have found in the prisoner quarters.

The next morning, Sid stayed behind when the bus left. He decided to keep an eye on the prison and see if he could pick up on anything. If he could stay out of Heglin's way, maybe the man would forget he was here and repeat his actions from yesterday morning. In a corner of his mind, Sid wondered if Heglin had put the soldiers up to that conversation last night. Surely if theft was the issue, Commander Moss would have mentioned it.

Sid strolled through the prisoner section, noting that everything seemed in place. The beds were neatly made, and the aisles clear of clothes and other personal belongings. As he reached the end of the first room, Sid was surprised to see a prisoner under his covers asleep. Nothing appeared wrong with the man other than he lounged in bed rather than worked his job.

Sid neared the bed, keeping his steps light. The man sprang

from his bed and grappled with Sid until he held Sid in a neck hold.

"You looking for something?" The words hissed into Sid's ear. "I told you come today. You take nothing more from my men and will return what you stole."

Sid pulled down on the arms locked around his throat. The man was stronger than he looked, and Sid grew light-headed. Someone said he'd been here? And he stole? That had Heglin's fingerprints all over it. But he couldn't get to the bottom of this while in a choke hold.

He tried to slide his foot behind the prisoner and knock him off his feet, but the man only pulled harder while lifting him off the ground. Sid scratched at the man's face and arms, but he seemed oblivious to any contact.

The man was a brute.

Why would Heglin set him up? What was he trying to cover up?

Sid licked his lips and tried to force some words out. "Stop. You'll be executed for killing an American soldier."

"I accept the punishment if it ends the stealing."

The man was beyond reason. Sid arched his back and lunged backward with everything in him. The prisoner grunted as Sid's full weight toppled on top of his, carrying them both to the floor. Sid felt the whoosh of air that left the man's lungs as they collided with the floor. His choke hold eased. Sid rolled to the side and rubbed his neck, keeping a wary eye on the prisoner.

Sid pulled a piece of rope from a bed frame and used it to tie the prisoner's hands together before he came around. The prisoner groaned and tried to roll over. He eased to a sitting position and hung his head.

"Who told you to wait for me?"

The prisoner shook his head, lips squeezed in a tight line.

"I will get to the bottom of this, so I suggest you tell me before I decide you tried to kill me." Sid's heart pounded. If the prisoner didn't decide to cooperate soon, he didn't want to know what he'd have to do to get answers. He took a deep breath and prayed for control. He needed some. Fast.

The prisoner stared at him, his face a mask. A muscle twitched in his jaw, but his eyes remained set.

"All right. You get to come with me." Sid hauled the man to his feet and dragged him up the stairs and to the office. Heglin had disappeared, so Sid marched into his office, shut the door behind them, and settled the prisoner in a chair. He slipped around the desk and grabbed the phone.

"Commander Moss, please." Sid tapped his foot as he waited. What should he tell the commander? That someone used a prisoner to try to harm him? That he didn't have any proof of who, just a few bruises?

"Good morning, sir. I'll bring one of the prisoners back with me. No, sir, I don't have any concrete answers yet. Yes, there are some strange things happening. But the prisoners seem well cared for. I'll stay another day or two and then return. Yes, sir." Sid hung up and stared at the prisoner. "What am I going to do with you for another couple of days?"

The man continued to ignore him.

"Guess you're my new shadow." Sid stood. "Let's get back to work."

The door opened as Sid reached for it. Heglin stood there, face rigid. "What are you doing in my office? With one of my prisoners?"

"Checked in with Commander Moss. And this prisoner is no longer yours. He attacked a U.S. soldier and will return to Camp Atlanta with me in a couple of days. I wonder about your security, Heglin. He shouldn't have stayed behind."

"The doctor determined he was too sick to work."

"Seems healthy as a horse now." Sid grabbed the prisoner's shoulder and pushed past Heglin.

The next two days passed with no concrete answers. Sid hiked over to the German center across the street and ate with some of the locals, met with the local doctor who worked with the prisoners, and generally kept his eyes and ears open. While things felt off, nothing jumped out as wrong.

He drove back to Camp Atlanta, with one prisoner and a truck full of questions, feeling as though he'd somehow failed.

Once he'd turned the prisoner over to the camp brig, he marched toward Commander Moss's office. He waited and waited and waited. Thoughts of what he'd rather do filtered through his mind. And a feisty blond kept cycling through his mind. Regardless of what happened next, he knew he needed to find Anna. Too much time had passed since he'd seen her.

That feeling seemed strange. What had happened to the guy who enjoyed the company of everybody? When had she sneaked so far under his radar that she demanded more from him? Yet he knew she would never actually do that.

No, she'd wait for him to make a decision and approach her. And if somebody else stole her affection during that time, it would be his loss alone. He couldn't let that happen. As soon as he was done with Commander Moss, he'd have to try to reach her at the Wisdoms'. The sound of her voice would have to be enough today.

But it wouldn't be forever.

twenty-two

Thursday afternoon, nausea roiled Anna's stomach as she approached Corporal Robertson. She hoped he'd be in a good mood since remnants of his lunch sat on his desk. Though everything in her fought what she had to do, she had no choice. Maybe if she did this, the knot that continued to tighten her stomach would finally ease.

"Corporal Robertson?" Her voice squeaked, and she cleared her throat.

He looked up, his mouth pressed into a slight frown. "Yes, Miss Goodman?"

"Could I speak with you a moment?" At his silence, she swallowed and rushed on. "I need a week to go home and make sure everything's okay. My papa isn't well, and it's a crucial time at the farm. If he's not caring for things, the crops could be lost."

"You've made a commitment to work here."

"Yes, sir. And I'll return. I need this time to take care of business at home. I'm not asking you to hold my job long. One week should be plenty of time." Anna crossed her fingers behind her back and waited.

He shuffled through some papers on his desk. "To keep your job, you'll need to back by the following Monday."

"Yes, sir. Thank you." She slipped from his office before he could change his mind.

That evening, the still July heat pressed Anna deeper into the chair she'd curled into. The Wisdoms' parlor stood empty, and usually she'd soak up the solitude. Instead, tonight the book she'd picked up couldn't hold her attention. Her thoughts kept returning to the conversation she'd had with Corporal Robertson that morning. She'd actually done it.

She'd made the decision, and now she had to find a way to survive the time. It would be easy to count down the days until she returned to her job and her steady existence here at the Wisdoms'.

She shook her head. It was too late to second-guess herself now. And what harm could come in nine days at home?

No, this was the right thing to do. That she knew full well. Now if her mind would quit arguing with her heart.

One good thing about going home—she might actually see more of the captivating Mr. Chance. Warmth cloaked her from the inside out and stole up her cheeks. She decided she liked that thought. Very much.

By Friday afternoon, even the thought of seeing Sid couldn't control the shivers that coursed through her body. The thought of staying all that time alone with her father would drive her crazy if she let it.

Dottie eased to a stop in front of the farmhouse. Anna tried to move, but every muscle in her body refused to cooperate. Sheer determination kept her lungs pulling air in and pushing it out.

"You don't have to do this." Dottie's soft voice pulled at Anna. "We can turn around and go back to Kearney. You know the Wisdoms won't mind."

Anna stared at the back door. If she didn't move, Papa would barge through it yelling orders and curses. She couldn't tear her eyes from it any more than she could fly away. She slowly shook her head.

Dottie reached for her hand and held it tight. "I'll pray for you. And you know Sid will come running the moment you ask."

A tear trickled down Anna's cheek. If only he were here now. She'd searched for the truck that often waited next to the barn on Friday afternoons, but the yard stood empty.

She took a deep breath and pulled her shoulders back. "Thanks for the ride." She leaned over and kissed Dottie on the cheek. "See you in a week."

"You can't get rid of me that easily. I'll be by Sunday." Dottie shrugged. "In case I miss you at church."

"Of course. Don't worry. I'll be fine." If only she believed her words. *Okay, Lord. I'm trying to do what You asked. Please be with me and give me the strength I'll need to survive the next week.*

Anna grabbed her bag out of the backseat and waved as Dottie pulled out of the yard. This time, Dottie missed the flowers as she backed out. Maybe it was a sign for the rest of the week.

After plopping the bag by the door, Anna walked toward the fields. She needed to see the progress. At least that excuse worked if needed. From the outside rows, it looked as if the prisoners had completed the detasseling. The wheat looked ready to explode from the kernels. She pulled a head off one stalk and popped the kernels out. She chewed on them until they gelled together and turned the consistency of gum.

She'd noticed that many surrounding fields that once held rows of winter wheat were now bare. Not one row at the Goodman farm had fallen. She'd need to get a ride to town and make sure the county extension officer knew they needed help. Now.

As she eyed the crop, she prayed they'd have time to get it in before a summer storm blew through.

❧

Sid glanced at his watch and winced. Everyone seemed to move slowly through the thick heat. A blast of humidity filled the air, adding to the discomfort.

While no one else seemed ready for the weekend, he was. A Class A pass waited for him, and he knew exactly what he would do with it. Head to Holdrege with a stop by the Goodman farm. He'd missed Anna each time he called the Wisdoms this week. He'd explode if he didn't talk to her soon.

That thought unsettled him. But he couldn't deny it.

As he'd thought and prayed this week, he'd decided he had

two options. One, run from any possible deepening of their relationship. Two, surrender and see what God might have in store.

He longed to fight the thought of surrender. How could that be what God had in mind? Yet he couldn't shake the idea that was exactly what God wanted him to do.

The line moved forward, and finally Sid walked out with his pass in one hand and keys to Trent's vehicle in the other. The miles passed in a blur as he raced the Ford to the Goodman farm. He didn't know what he'd say to Mr. Goodman if Anna wasn't there. The detasseling completed, he didn't have any business stopping by. And he didn't think Mr. Goodman would welcome his company—not that he looked forward to seeing Mr. Goodman, either.

He flipped on his blinker and eased into the driveway. No vehicle waited, so either Dottie had already dropped Anna off, or Anna wasn't coming home.

A suitcase leaned against the house. He parked and hopped out of the car. A flash of color caught his eye, and his heart lifted. She'd come home, after all.

&

Anna turned back toward the house. She couldn't delay the inevitable any longer. A rumble caught her ear, and she turned to see a Ford coupe pull in front of the house. Her hand fluttered to her neck as she waited to see who sat in the vehicle.

A tall soldier sauntered from the car toward her. Her breath caught in her throat. He'd come out to the farm, after all. Her thoughts jumbled together, and she stood as if struck dumb. How could one man have such an effect on her?

A lazy grin carved Sid's face as he approached. "Hey, Anna."

"Hello."

"I didn't know if I'd see you."

She nodded. "I decided I needed to come home for a while. Make sure the crop got in."

"Your dad will be glad to see you."

"I don't know about that."

"He'll be glad to see anyone but me and the prisoners." Sid stood toe-to-toe with her.

The scent of his cologne reached her, and she could almost taste the cloves. He grabbed her hand and rubbed a thumb across her fingers.

"Come have dinner with me?"

Anna nodded, and warmth exploded through her. "I'd like that. But I have to check on Papa and see to the chores first."

"You might be surprised."

"Why?"

"I've actually caught him outside the house a few times."

She tried to focus on his words even as her attention wandered to their interlocked hands.

"A couple of his friends came out and had him doing all kinds of things. They seemed to be a good influence on him."

She chuckled at his words. Who would do something like that? She couldn't picture others leading Papa to do something he didn't want to do. "So who were they?"

"Who?"

"These two miracle workers."

Sid shrugged. "Teddy and Gus, I think. They did a good job with him." His Adam's apple bobbed. "So will you have dinner with me, or are you delaying?"

A warm feeling engulfed Anna. The usually self-assured Sid Chance stood almost undone in her presence. She grinned at him. "Race you to milk Nellie. The winner chooses our dinner location."

Anna sprinted toward the barn and laughed over her shoulder when she caught Sid languishing behind. "You're supposed to race, silly."

"Oh, I'm all too happy to let you milk the cow." The goofy look on his face warned that he had other thoughts on his mind. Heat crept up her cheeks, and she hurried ahead. He could play whatever games he wanted. They were too old for silliness.

As the chores passed in a blur of laughter and games, she wondered if maybe she'd forgotten how to have a good time. Maybe the fight to keep everything going had stolen the joy from her days. The words of Psalm 103:2 washed across her mind: *"Bless the LORD, O my soul, and forget not all His benefits."* When was the last time she'd taken the time to consider everything He'd done for her rather than count up a laundry list of things she needed to handle? And when had she invited Him to help her with that laundry list? Why did she feel such a need to take the burden on her shoulders?

Sid approached her and grabbed her hands. "Where did you go?"

She lowered her gaze. "God was reminding me it's okay to celebrate the little things. Like beating you at chores."

His eyebrows arched. "I think it's time you picked your dinner spot."

She tugged, trying to free her hands. "All right. Let's head up to the house. Don't forget the basket with eggs."

Sid reached for the basket but refused to let go of one hand. "So we're staying here?"

"Simple fare on a simple farm." If he wanted to tease her like that, he would do it on her turf. And having Papa around would surely keep Sid in check.

"Then I'll have to steal my kiss now." Sid pulled her closer to him, and she found herself staring into his eyes. One could get lost exploring the depths of them. Emotion flashed through them before a guard fell. "You aren't playing fair, Anna."

"What?" Confusion clouded her thoughts as he pushed her away.

"Why do you insist on knowing me?"

"Isn't that how it's supposed to be? You know my fears and joys, and I know yours."

He grunted. Then pulled her back into the circle of his arms. "This is what I want you remembering." His lips closed on hers, and Anna sank into his embrace for a moment.

When she almost couldn't breathe, she pushed her palms

against his chest. "You can't do that, Sid. Either you want to know me, or you don't. You have to decide." She spun on her heel, grabbed her suitcase, and entered the house, cheeks flaming.

twenty-three

The truck ground across the country road, its bed loaded with prisoners. The county extension officer had assigned this group to return to the Goodman farm to harvest the winter wheat. Days like this, Sid longed to return to Fort Robinson and the simplicity of training men and dogs. That job seemed so much easier than navigating farming and the mind of a certain young woman.

He hadn't known whether to laugh or groan when the powers that be determined he should return to that farm. He'd spent the days and nights since Friday plagued by Anna Goodman. Her blond curls and pert nose haunted him. Why did she impact him this way? And why did one kiss make him feel like such a louse?

She was a puzzle that could drive him crazy. He couldn't decide how he felt about that.

"So are you turning or driving all day? Gas is a premium product, you know." Trent's teasing pulled Sid from his thoughts.

"Maybe I'll let you drive next time."

"And the moon will turn green. You aren't willing to give up control. Even to someone dependable like me."

Trent's words hit him in the chest like a machine gun blast. Was that his problem? He couldn't give up control? He wanted things his way or not at all? The words settled on him like a spotlight illuminating a corner of his heart he didn't think he wanted to examine.

"Yeah, well, I suppose it's time to get these fellas to work."

"Another day, another wage. I'll never understand how grateful they are to work."

"Eliminates boredom and lets them do something important."

Trent snorted. "Not so sure why doctors and engineers

think farming is important. Especially when it's for the enemy."

Sid held his tongue. While he enjoyed hanging out with Trent, there were times that his opinions closely bordered those of some of the other guards. The prisoners were men, plain and simple. As such, they deserved respect. Most of the time they received it. But some of the biases boggled his mind.

And those biases traveled over to the civilians. Nebraska had a large German population, immigrants who were now in the second or third generation. Yet many of them had taken to hiding their German heritage in fear of reprisals like the Japanese Americans experienced.

Sid pulled the truck to a stop in front of the Goodman barn. Three men stood in a semicircle, watching. It looked as though Mr. Goodman had decided today made a good day to get out of the house. His cohorts stood on each side of him. Gus and Teddy, the men working a miracle in the old bear.

"Mr. Goodman." Sid reached out to shake his hand. "Good morning, sir. Gus. Teddy. I've got prisoners ready to bring in the wheat."

"We could have used you a week or two ago."

"Yes, sir. We finished the detasseling, and the prisoners were assigned to another farm last week. The county agent didn't assign us until this week. The prisoners go where he indicates." No need to mention where he'd been last week.

"Humph." Mr. Goodman turned to his friends. "Do you think these men can be taught?"

"Now, Ed, you know they can. You've seen how hard they work and how eager to learn they are. Don't you think it's time to forget what happened to you in the Great War?"

Mr. Goodman's face soured. "I'm out here, ain't I? What more do you want?"

"An attitude change, but we'll take what we can get." Gus rubbed his ample belly. "Let's get to work while there's daylight."

Teddy nodded. "I've got the threshing equipment all set up."

Sid watched the two older men get the prisoners settled into groups. Mr. Goodman watched from the side. Sid wondered if he'd ever learn the full story, but at least Mr. Goodman had left the house and wasn't holding a gun to the prisoners' heads. He also hadn't sensed any alcohol on the man's breath. Come to think of it, he hadn't noticed that for a few visits. It was a start.

He looked to the house, noticing the curtains billowing out through the open kitchen windows. The scent of something sweet and spicy drifted on the wind.

"She's still here, boy."

Were his thoughts that transparent? Based on the grin covering Mr. Goodman's face, they must be. *Looks like more than his attitude toward the Germans has softened.* Sid wasn't sure what had caused the change, but he'd take it.

Mr. Goodman looked toward the house. "Anna said she's here through the harvest, so you might want to drag things out a bit."

Or speed them up. Sid didn't know how many more encounters with her he'd survive.

The morning in the fields sped by, and when the sun stood high in the sky, the bell by the back door pealed. The Germans straggled out of the fields, many looking drained by the heat and labor. They perked up when they reached the back door and found blankets spread in the shade of the oak trees. A table stood by the door, laden down with sandwiches, apples, and glasses of fresh milk.

The men loaded chipped plates before collapsing on the blankets. In minutes, the food disappeared, followed by quiet snores as the prisoners lay down. One pulled a slim book from his pocket and flipped its pages.

Sid leaned against the truck, watching Anna avoid him. Anytime she caught him looking at her, color bloomed across her cheeks. She had no idea how beautiful she was as she served the men. She seemed to have settled whatever had weighed her mind down about having prisoners on the farm.

Maybe the money issue had been resolved. It must have been if she chose to stay here rather than hurry back to Kearney and her cash job.

She disappeared into the house with the last empty platter. He pushed off the truck, ready to follow her, until Gus stood and roused the prisoners. Time to head back to the field.

"You got them, Trent?"

"Sure, lover boy. Don't take too long." A gleam sparked in Trent's eyes as he laughed.

Sid strode to the door and knocked. He opened it and slipped inside.

Blond curls had escaped Anna's headband and ringed her face, begging to be touched. She stepped back when she saw him.

"What can I help you with, Specialist Chance? Need more food?"

He shook his head. "I wanted to see you."

She backed into the sink and crossed her arms. "Not sure I want to see you."

"Sure you do. Your cheeks turn a beautiful shade when you see me." He stepped closer. "Can we start again?"

"Why would we want to do that?"

"Because you are a beautiful woman who I care about."

"You have interesting ways of showing that, mister." A twinkle filled her eyes, and he relaxed in response. She might be mad, but she'd play along.

"So maybe I stepped out of line Friday."

"Maybe?" She snorted. "Definitely."

"So give me another chance." He tugged one of her hands free. "I promise to be a perfect gentleman."

"Frankly, I don't think you have it in you." She considered him carefully, searching his eyes until he thought she must see every last corner of his soul. "If you can manage to be a gentleman the rest of this week, then we can go out on Friday or Saturday. But you might want to make sure the wheat's in by then."

"Why?"

"If a storm blows up while it's in the field, that will end any chance of a night out."

"All right, young lady. You win. I'll hurry back to the field and bring the wheat in myself if I have to."

"See that you do." She stepped closer. "I'd like that time with you very much."

He leaned in for a quick peck on the cheek. "See, I can be a perfect gentleman."

She shooed him away with a towel, but he left whistling a wordless tune filled with promise.

❧

The week flew for Anna. Tending to the chores and providing food for the men filled her days. Fortunately, they appreciated the sustenance no matter how many times she offered hard-boiled eggs and fresh bread.

The crop came in as big as it looked, giving the farm a chance to turn the corner this year. The knots of tension lining Anna's neck eased each time she thought of that. Maybe, just maybe, next year could start with a little money in the bank rather than robbing Peter to pay Paul. And the corn remained in the field, where it stood tall, soaking in the sunshine.

By Friday, the prisoners had cut down the wheat, threshed most of it, and stored the precious kernels in the silo. Next week, a truck from the co-op would come collect the crop.

Another year or two like this, and the farm might join the 1940s with a tractor. Gus had managed to sweet-talk one of the neighboring farmers out of his for a couple of days, and it had amazed Anna to watch the wheat fall in short order.

It looked as though Sid would get his night out. And she had to admit she looked forward to it. Maybe he'd even act like a gentleman. No, she kind of liked him with his rakish air like Rhett Butler. She had a feeling it remained an act, but she'd play along as long as he honored her lines.

It felt good to slip into a dress after a week in work clothes. Maybe someday she'd have a job that allowed her to dress up each day. Until then, she'd enjoy every moment of rare opportunities like tonight.

Sid's whistle drifting through the open window announced his arrival. Anna pinched her cheeks in the small vanity mirror and then hurried to the living room. Papa had already welcomed him in with a sturdy handshake. She marveled at the change that had come over Papa in the last week. The more time he spent with the prisoners, the less they seemed to bother him. Maybe he'd decided the time had come to let go of the pain from twenty-five years earlier. His limp even seemed less pronounced.

"So where's that beautiful daughter of yours, sir?"

"Primping in her room."

Anna stayed in the shadows while Papa brought Sid into the living room.

"Ah, there she is. You'd better be good to her, son. She's all I've got left."

Sid's face softened when he saw her. His eyes widened, and he stretched out a hand for a chair. "I'll do that. Yes, sirree, I'll take very good care of her."

Papa chuckled. "Be sure that you do. She'll demand nothing less from you."

"We'll be back soon, Papa."

"See that you are. There's still plenty of work to do tomorrow."

There always was, but as she looked into Sid's eyes, saw the deep appreciation hidden in them, she didn't care. She would enjoy every moment of their time together.

He took her hand. A jolt shot up her arm. She almost pulled back. The last thing they needed was more energy between them. No, they needed time to prove their relationship was grounded on more than goose bumps.

As Sid led her to the car, she couldn't wait to explore the future.

twenty-four

July melted into August, the heat unrelenting, interrupted only by short periods of rain. Anna had returned to Kearney safe in the knowledge that Papa seemed well on the road back to himself.

While she'd been home, one of the prisoners had approached her about helping with costumes for a musical. Now one corner of her room at the Wisdoms' bore the results. Bolts of cloth cluttered the area. Sid had promised to help her, but unless he could find little elves to sew costumes in the middle of the night, she didn't know what he could do.

A sigh slipped out, and she slumped on the edge of her bed. Someday she must learn to say no.

"Staring at it won't turn that lump of material into whatever it's supposed to become." Dottie stood against the door, her arms crossed.

"You must think I'm crazy."

"Maybe a little. They must have done a great job with the harvest."

"I was grateful. We'll make it through the winter now." Anna shrugged. "Staring at it won't make it go away. Let's cart the first bolt downstairs."

Before long, fabric covered the dining-room table, and several boarders gathered around to help. Anna was grateful that it didn't bother anyone that the costumes were for the prisoners to use in one of their plays. Instead, the gals treated it like a social event. Before long, Mrs. Wisdom brought some of her famous snickerdoodle cookies and lemonade. That week, many evenings passed in a blur of laughter and flying needles as the gals cleared the table after dinner and Anna brought the fabric and patterns back down. After a week, the bolts of cloth had turned into costumes needing only buttons and finishing details.

Thursday, Sid called with the message that he'd pick her up Friday night to take her to Camp Atlanta to deliver the costumes. Her heart fluttered at the thought of dinner afterward. Then back to the farm for a weekend interrupted only by the show on Saturday evening. Somehow, it sounded like a perfect weekend. She hoped Sid would take her to the show, too.

"Dottie, do you mind me going with Sid?"

"Don't be silly. I think I'll actually relax here for the weekend." Dottie lounged on her bed, arms locked behind her head. "It seemed to work well for you, and I can't stay if I'm carting you home."

Anna's mouth dropped open. She grabbed the pillow from her bed and threw it at Dottie. "I can't believe you said that."

Dottie's eyes flashed as she launched to her feet. "Time for you to stand on your own two feet, darling. I think Sid will be good for that."

"You are impossible." Anna covered her mouth to stifle nervous laughter. "Time will tell what becomes of the two of us."

"Just remember to invite me to the wedding." Dottie flounced out of the room with a big grin.

Anna shook her head, grabbed another shirt, and thrust it into her bag. Before she was ready, Dottie ran back upstairs to tell her that Sid was waiting. Together, the girls wrestled bags of costumes down and dropped them at his feet.

"Think you can get them in your car, soldier?"

Sid's eyes got big as he looked at the piles. "How many costumes did you make?"

"As many as they requested. Let's get going. I can't wait to see their faces."

The expression on Sid's face indicated he couldn't, either. Why did he look as if he'd swallowed something incredibly sour? Anna pushed the thought from her mind as they hopped in the car. As the miles ticked by, Sid loosened up.

Conversation flowed freely, mixed with lots of laughter, and before she was ready, Camp Atlanta came into view and he slowed the car.

"Now don't be surprised if the prisoners are. . .hesitant around you. They aren't used to seeing many civilians here."

"It will be fine. They asked for my help, after all." Anna bounced out of the car when it finally pulled to a stop in front of a long, narrow concrete building. She glanced around. All the buildings had the look of standard government-issue structures built in a hurry.

This particular building had posters on the outside in German and English. Looked like a community hall. A prisoner exited dressed in his denim outfit with the painted Ps and Ws. He stopped in his tracks when he saw Sid.

"Sir?"

"Luka. Miss Goodman has a car full of costumes for you." The funny look returned to Sid's face as he spoke.

Luka cocked his head and looked from Anna to the car. "Costumes?"

"Yes, one of you asked her to help. She took that to heart."

Luka disappeared into the building and came back out with several men. In no time, they had the car unloaded. Quiet German comments passed between them as they worked, but Anna couldn't understand any of it.

"Thank you for your help." Luka nodded in a bow. "Please come to show."

"You're welcome." Anna looked at Sid. "Can I come? To the show?"

"I can bring you if you like. Tomorrow night, Luka?"

"Yes, sir. Six." Luka bowed again and slipped into the building.

Anna linked arms with Sid. "Sounds like we have a date, then."

"How did I get lucky enough to spend so much time with you?"

Sid settled her in the car. Anna marveled at the change

that only a week had brought into their friendship. Maybe it would work out, after all. Her heart skipped at the thought.

દ⊱

Sid tried hard to wipe the smirk off his face before he climbed back in the car. Who in their right mind thought the prisoners would need twenty copies of the exact same costume? Sid had no idea what entertainment the men planned for tomorrow night, but this would be interesting to see.

The evening passed quietly at the Goodman farm. They'd fallen into a routine of completing the chores together and then enjoying a quiet meal with Anna's father. Mr. Goodman even brought out checkers when they'd finished the meal. Sid kept an eye open for alcohol, but it looked as though Mr. Goodman had put it away. Maybe getting back to the work of the farm had been the cure all along.

"Mr. Goodman, thanks for the game of checkers. It's been awhile since someone trounced me."

Mr. Goodman grinned. "You can always learn something from your elders, boy."

"Yes, sir. I need to get back to camp. See me to the door, Anna?" Sid stood. Her soft smile stilled a place deep inside him.

"I'll be back in a minute, Papa."

Mr. Goodman nodded and picked up his paper. Sid must have made progress if the man didn't feel the need to watch them through the window.

The screen door slammed behind them, and he pulled Anna against him. "I'll be back tomorrow late afternoon to pick you up."

She nodded then relaxed next to him. He tipped her chin up, searching her eyes in the glow from the windows. They were filled with gentleness and a spark of something. He leaned toward her and waited, but she didn't pull away. He closed the distance for a soft kiss then stepped back, taking a deep breath. "Till tomorrow."

She smiled and watched as he pulled out of the driveway.

Saturday afternoon he collected Anna and took her to

Holdrege for an early dinner. They strolled the streets of downtown, enjoying the cool breeze. The sounds of a violin's soft wail drew them to a store. Anna peeked in the window of the pawnshop.

"Let's go in."

Sid pulled open the door, and they stepped inside. Stale cigar smoke mixed with mint tickled his nose. Old Mr. Gustave, the proprietor, leaned against the counter, fingers tapping a beat on the counter. Two Germans stood in the shop with a guard behind them. One of the prisoners held a violin and played the instrument with a passion that made it sing. Anna leaned into Sid and sighed as she listened.

"That's beautiful."

Sid had to agree. The man had turned a lump of wood into a songbird. After listening a few minutes, they continued back to the car. They made it back to Camp Atlanta in time to catch the show. The prisoners had used the costumes to add humor to their vaudeville-style act. Anna soaked in the show with enthusiasm. Sid watched her out of the corner of his eye. Did she ever do anything halfheartedly? He hadn't seen any evidence that she did.

They strolled out of the building, Anna humming one of the tunes. He looked down at her, and his heart stopped. Why could he now imagine walking like this until they were hunched and gray? He rubbed her hand with his thumb.

"How would you like to have dessert at the Officer's Club?"

Anna stopped humming and nodded. "I'd like that. Am I dressed appropriately?"

"Hmm. Let me check."

She twirled in front of him, hand posed under her chin. Her blue skirt swished around her knees, and the color enhanced her eyes.

"I can't think of anything better."

A soft blush colored her cheeks, only heightening her beauty. "Thank you." She reclaimed his arm. "Lead on."

It took a few minutes, but too soon they reached the Officer's Club. He opened the door, and she glided past him into the entryway.

"Looky here. If it ain't the German-loving soldier."

Sid stopped inside the doorway, trying to decide how to respond. Should he let it go? More and more of these remarks were fired his way, and he'd grown weary of them. Anna held her breath by his side. Her fingers tightened on his arm, and when he looked down, he saw that her knuckles were white.

"Cat got your tongue, Chance? Or do you only understand German?"

Sid threw back his shoulders and tugged Anna to follow. "Let's go find a table away from the rabble."

She nodded, lips pressed together. She bobbled on the first step, and he held her firmly.

"Guess he's too good to talk to us. Maybe if we were PWs, that would change." Larry Heglin stood in front of Sid, an ugly leer on his face. "So is she German, too?"

Sid clenched his hands to keep from punching Larry. It took every ounce of control not to jump the man. "Don't ever speak about Miss Goodman that way again, Heglin. You can say whatever you want about me, but leave her out of this."

"Ever the noble one, aren't you? Someday you'll slip, and I'll be there, spreading the word." Heglin brushed past Sid as he pushed through the door.

Sid glanced at Anna. "Are you okay?" She nodded her head, but her chin trembled. "Let's get you in and settled. Don't worry about Larry. Men like him are all talk. You learn to ignore them until they have something meaningful to say."

Anna relaxed when she sank into a seat. Sid started talking, regaling her with stories until the shadows left her gaze. He'd shelter her for a lifetime if she'd let him.

twenty-five

The sunlight tickled Anna's nose, pulling her from a dream she didn't want to leave. In it, Sid defended her from others, his eyes alight with love and concern. She squeezed her eyes shut and curled around her pillow.

The clock ticked a metronome's beat in her ear until she finally groped for it. She squinted at it and groaned.

Time to get up and get ready for church. She'd join the Wisdoms at their community church today, then head to the air base for the Labor Day picnic. She'd mentioned the picnic to Sid, but he hadn't taken the hint. Guess she'd go alone.

The church service passed in a blur, with the pastor preaching on Psalm 103:2. Everywhere she turned, it seemed God reminded her to pay attention to everything He'd done for her. With each day, she could see His movement in her life, and gratitude bubbled inside her. The Wisdoms dropped her off at the air base after the service.

"Will you be able to get back home all right?" Mr. Wisdom pulled Anna's picnic basket from the rumble seat and handed it to her.

"I'll catch the bus. Thanks again." Anna adjusted the beret resting on her curls and waved as the Wisdoms pulled away from the gate. Picking up the basket, she smiled at the guards and strolled to the other side.

The grounds buzzed with more activity than usual as cars zipped to the parade grounds. Anna joined the flow of people, feeling incredibly alone.

"Anna, over here."

Anna scanned the crowd, trying to locate the person yelling for her. Finally, she spied someone waving. She raised a hand to shield the sun and smiled. Francie Miller waved

151

from a group of her coworkers. Anna waited for a car to pass then hurried across the street.

"Morning, gals."

"So you ventured out for the shindig." Francie smiled and hooked arms with Anna.

Anna nodded. "It was a good weekend to stay in town."

"Let's find a place to settle down and eat. I'm starved." In no time, Francie had the group of girls settled on a couple of blankets. They broke into their baskets and spread out the food, a buffet of choices.

Once she'd filled her plate with fried chicken and potato and other salads, Anna settled on a blanket and soaked in the carefree banter. A military band struck up a rousing march, and the crowd clapped along. Local politicians and officers took turns making speeches. As the afternoon wore on, Anna's eyes grew heavy. If things didn't change soon, she'd fall asleep to the droning voices.

She slipped her hat off her hair and fanned her face. Anything to wake up.

Corporal Robertson stepped up to the podium, and the microphone squealed. He tapped it and then shrugged. "Good afternoon, ladies and gentlemen. It is a pleasure to add my personal welcome. As we celebrate Labor Day, I wanted to take a moment to recognize one individual who works in my department.

"In the parachute department, we have instituted what I like to call the Cocoon Club. It is an exclusive club. Only people who have packed a parachute which later saved someone's life can be inducted into this group. To date, about one dozen of your fellow residents have had the honor of saving someone's life by completing their jobs diligently and competently."

He rubbed a hand across his cheek and shrugged. "None of the members strive for recognition, and that certainly remains true of the newest member. She works hard every day and focuses completely on the task at hand.

"Two weeks ago, I received a letter from a captain thanking me for the excellent job with his parachute. He flew a bomber behind enemy lines hours before the attack on Normandy launched. However, the Germans hit his plane with shrapnel and antiaircraft fire. As a result, he and the rest of his crew were forced to bail out over enemy territory. A parachute of a crew member failed to open, but his performed as expected.

"He spent two months as a prisoner of war before escaping and rejoining American troops three weeks ago. The first thing he did was post a letter to us expressing his appreciation. Captain Brent Goodman's parachute was packed by his sister, Anna Goodman. Anna, please join me up here as we welcome you to the Cocoon Club."

Anna tried to pull in a breath of air, but her lungs had frozen at the mention of Brent's name. He had escaped from the Germans! All this time they'd thought him a prisoner, and he'd fought to find his way back.

The crowd erupted into applause. She clamped one hand around her stomach in a desperate grip as her other hand covered her mouth. Tears poured down her cheeks, and her colleagues wrapped her in warm hugs.

"Anna." Corporal Robertson tapped his foot as he stared her direction.

A veil of tears tried to blind her. She didn't have the strength to stand, let alone to walk in front of the crowd. A hand covered her shoulder. She could tell by the strength it offered that Sid had found her.

"I'll help you up there." His voice held a note of strength mixed with compassion.

At his words, her tears turned into sobs. She leaned into Sid's shoulder and cried as if her heart would never recover. He ran a hand over her hair and whispered words she couldn't understand. The applause slowed, and Anna heard the rustle of people standing to their feet.

Sid brushed hair behind her ear and leaned close. "I think

they're determined to see this dynamo who saved her brother's life."

Anna nodded and wiped the tears from her face. She could do this. All it entailed was walking to the podium and shaking Corporal Robertson's hand. Sid helped her to her feet then guided her through the crowd. Anna kept her gaze fixed on his shoulder, sure that if she looked at anyone else, she'd erupt in fresh tears. God was so good! Her brother had made it back, though after she got through giving him grief for letting her find out like this, he might wish he'd stayed hidden a bit longer.

"Come on up here, Anna." Corporal Robertson helped her onto the stage. "Congratulations on saving a man's life. Keep up the good work." He leaned close. "Take tomorrow off if you need to. I didn't realize you didn't know he'd escaped."

"Thank you, sir." She slipped down before he could ask her to do anything else. All she wanted to do was go home and make sure Papa knew. She turned to Sid as soon as both feet were back on solid ground. "Can you take me home?" She sucked in a shuddering breath, and fresh tears washed down her cheeks. "I need to tell Papa."

Sid studied her face a moment then nodded. "Follow me."

With Sid navigating her through the field of well-wishers, they reached his car in short order. The trip to the farm passed in a cloud of conflicting emotions. Thankfulness dominated her jumbled thoughts. Only God could have protected Brent through everything and helped him find his way back to the Allies.

She stumbled from the car before Sid braked. "Papa. Papa! Come here."

Should she run to the barn to look for him? Or was he in the house? Her mind couldn't get instructions to her legs. She couldn't decide whether to sink into Papa's arms or spin and shout the good news at the top of her lungs.

The slamming of the screen door caught her attention.

"What is it, girl? You aren't hurt, are you?"

"No, Papa." She gulped in air but felt like she sucked it through a straw.

"Well, spit it out."

"Brent. He's—"

"He's what?"

She took a deep breath and let the joy explode from her. "He's safe. He's back with the Allies."

Papa pulled her into his arms then slapped Sid on the back. "My boy's coming home."

As she watched his exuberance, Anna knew everything would be all right.

❧

Camp Atlanta seemed mundane to Sid after watching Anna tell her father that Brent lived. Yet Sid tried to focus on the task at hand. With the corn harvest a few weeks away, the farmers needed the prisoners less, so more of his time drifted by watching prisoners who didn't want to escape. He supposed he should be grateful he had a posting like this when so many experienced battle firsthand. But boredom brought its own struggles. The lone highlight on many of his days was a call to Anna in the evening or the occasional opportunity to see her at the farm. Unfortunately, now that her father had come alive, she didn't spend every weekend back home.

The September days felt mired in molasses. One evening late in the month, Sid joined the others in their barracks. Trent sprawled across the bunk next to his, and they played a game of cards using the floor between their beds as a table. Before long, someone turned the lights out, and Sid tried to settle in.

He woke when something tickled his nose. It smelled as if someone had set a campfire outside the building. The smoky smell made his stomach grumble, and he thought about nights spent around a campfire. Maybe someone could find some marshmallows, graham crackers, and chocolate.

A pounding caused Sid to sit up.

"What's with all the racket?" Trent's raspy voice penetrated the silence.

"Looks like someone wants us up."

"Well, you go check. I'm in the middle of a great dream." Trent rolled over and pulled the covers tight against his chin.

The pounding continued. "Get up. You must get out now." The voice bore a heavy accent, and one of the soldiers cursed.

"If this is some kind of joke, someone will pay."

Sid sighed as he climbed out of bed. "And if it's not, you'll be sorry you didn't respond." He plodded to the door and opened it. He paused when he saw one of his prisoners standing there. "What do you need, Oskar?"

"Hurry. Must get out. Fire on building." He gestured wildly around the corner. "Come. Now."

Sid hurried to follow the man. He turned the corner and spotted a dozen prisoners in a line of sorts throwing buckets of water on a fire that lapped at the building. Dashing back into the barracks, he ran up and down the aisle, pulling blankets from the men.

"Everyone out now. The barracks are on fire."

The men launched out of their beds and hopped into pants, pulled on shirts.

An hour later, water had quenched the fire. A bedraggled group of prisoners and soldiers collapsed on the ground. Other soldiers straggled out of their barracks.

"What happened here?"

Sid looked up to see Commander Moss approaching. Even in the middle of the night, he wore his uniform and looked ready for an inspection.

"There was a fire, but a group of prisoners smelled it and came to put it out. They also alerted us so we were able to get out. It looks like the building will be fine, though we'll need to sleep somewhere else until the smoke clears."

Commander Moss turned to the prisoners. "Thank you for what you did tonight. I won't forget it." He turned to one of the officers. "Please escort them back to their building and make sure they are allowed to sleep late into the morning."

"Thank you, sir." Oskar spoke for the others. "We do

anything for Officer Chance."

At his words, Sid felt warmth spread through him. The prisoners appreciated his efforts on their behalf. The occasional ribbing from other soldiers amounted to nothing compared to what the prisoners had done. He couldn't wait to tell Anna about this. A yawn stretched his face. First, he needed some sleep. Then he'd find her.

twenty-six

The first nip of fall tinged the air, but the hint of a looming Indian summer promised that fall hadn't officially arrived. Anna sat on the Wisdoms' front step and hoped it would arrive in time for the corn harvest. She'd already arranged to spend that week home, helping with meals and anything else Papa needed.

She marveled at the changes in him. Since she'd told him that Brent had made it back to the Allies, he'd dived back into the farm. He didn't need her there on weekends to hold his hand and finish chores. Instead, the weekends were often filled with good-natured ribbing when Gus and Teddy came for dinner. They'd josh and tell tall tales with Papa until long after Anna gave up and went to bed.

With one breath she felt nothing but relief. Other times she wondered if he needed her at all anymore. She couldn't imagine finding her only purpose at the air base. Little remained for her at home, and a curious emptiness gnawed her.

The screech of the front door opening pulled Anna from her thoughts.

"Anna." Mrs. Wisdom stepped onto the porch. "You've got a phone call. Sounds like your soldier."

Warmth replaced the uneasiness that had surrounded her. It amazed her that the mere thought of Sid could do that. "Thank you." Anna followed Mrs. Wisdom inside and into the kitchen.

"Hello."

"Anna, are you free tonight?"

She paused as if checking her full calendar. "I could squeeze time in for you."

How was it possible to hear him smile across the phone?

"I won't have long, but let's grab a piece of pie somewhere."

"I think we have some left from dinner. Mrs. Wisdom won't mind if we eat it."

"Sounds even better. I'll be there in twenty minutes." Sid rang off, and Anna rushed up the stairs to her room.

Dottie lounged on her bed reading a book. "What's the hurry?"

"Sid's coming over."

A knowing smile curved Dottie's lips. "That explains it. Let me try to do something with that impossible hair." Anna sat down on the floor and handed Dottie a hairbrush. "Do you think Sid feels for you anything close to what you feel for him?"

Anna sighed. That was the question that plagued her when they were apart. She hoped, even prayed that he did. If he didn't, she wasn't sure what she would do. Her heart felt entwined with his.

❧

Sid drove the truck across Kearney to the Wisdoms'. His heart raced at the thought of seeing Anna, even if for a few minutes, and he wondered if that was good. She filled his thoughts and drove him to distraction. He couldn't imagine living the rest of his life without her. Spending time with her made him want to be a better man, someone she could honor. No one else drew that out of him.

Maybe she was the one. He had prayed about it. But he'd also decided they needed to spend time together, build their friendship, and see what their relationship contained. Maybe in her mind, he would forever be a nice soldier she once knew.

That wasn't enough for him. He wanted more. But he wanted it in God's timing.

And no matter how he prayed, he hadn't received the freedom to move ahead. Not yet. Hard as it was, he'd wait for that release.

That didn't mean he had to stay away, though. As he pulled up to the Wisdoms' home and saw Anna waiting on the front porch, his heart caught in his throat.

He couldn't imagine being anywhere else than gazing into those amazing blue eyes and hearing her heart.

❧

September rolled into October, and Anna returned to the farm for the week of the corn harvest. Storm clouds threatened on the horizon, and the radio carried word that the fields to the south were being pounded by rain. Anna prayed the storms would keep to the south or disappear altogether until after harvest. She hated the thought that the rain could devastate any crop.

Papa paced the house, pausing at each window to swipe the curtain aside and stare at the sky. Occasionally a curse would escape his lips, followed by a quick apology and a prayer for protection.

"Please sit down, Papa. You're driving me crazy with your constant pacing." Anna pulled the coffeepot off the stove. "I've brewed some fresh coffee. Sit down, and I'll pour you a cup."

"I don't need something to add to my jitters." Papa harrumphed and took a seat. Anna handed him a mug then watched as his fingers laced and unlaced around the cup. Back and forth in a gesture that telegraphed his fear.

She settled down next to him and placed a hand over his. "Papa, we can't do anything about the storm but pray. Maybe God will send it around us."

"Or maybe He'll send it right through here. It can join the other storms." He bowed his head, and Anna didn't know if he'd ever seemed so defeated. "Girl, I don't know how many more hits we can survive."

"God has seen us through so much, He won't leave us now. And we'll fight to keep the farm for Brent. If we have to let it go at some point, God will have something else in mind for us. You have to believe that."

Papa shook his head and stood. "I'm going to walk the fields."

Anna watched him leave and prayed that God would push the storm away. Papa might not survive another test.

The next morning, the sound of large raindrops pounding the windowpanes jerked Anna from sleep. She hurried out of bed to the window and brushed the curtain aside. Puddles stood in the yard. How had she not heard the storm during the night? She grabbed her robe and hurried to the kitchen. Papa sat at the kitchen table, head in his hands, a bottle of whiskey next to his mug of coffee.

Anna scurried toward him and grabbed the whiskey before he could look up. "Papa, no."

A dark scowl covered his face as he stared at her. "Leave it be, girl. What else am I supposed to do?"

"It's rain. It'll end, and the clouds will clear. Soon we'll be in the fields anyway."

"This is Nebraska. It's practically Columbus Day, and we could have a hard freeze before we get back in those fields."

"Can we do anything about it?" She waited. "I didn't think so. Your choice is to start drinking again or trust God."

Papa sagged against the table. "I can't do this on my own."

"Good. That's exactly where God wants us. Recognizing that life is more than we can handle on our own without Him." Anna took the bottle to the sink and set it down. "Papa, I can't worry about you when I'm in Kearney. You have to choose to stay sober. Mama would want it, but you have to do it. I'll go get dressed and handle the chores."

Anna slopped through the rain and puddles to take care of the cow and chickens. By midmorning, the rain had stopped. It would take days to dry, and as soon as it did, they could hurry into the fields.

She returned to the house with hesitant steps. What if Papa had picked up the bottle of whiskey, after all? Instead, she found him poring over material on soybeans.

"Maybe it's time to try something new. I've heard good things about soybeans."

Anna nodded. "Could be a welcome change for the land."

"Don't worry, Anna." He looked at her with hope in his eyes. "We'll make it. Gus came out to tell me that we'll have his corn harvester as soon as the fields dry. I was afraid we'd lost our window, but he'll take care of it."

"Then we won't need prisoners to get the crop in?"

"We'll let the machines do the heavy work, but we'll need them, too. It'll be a record harvest once the water drains."

Papa plotted out plans on a piece of paper as he pored over the brochures. For the first time in a long while, she believed him. The farm would make it regardless of the weather. And if Papa was fine, maybe she should start planning her future.

twenty-seven

The congregation sang the closing words of "Trust and Obey" as Sid slipped into the pew next to Anna and her father. The corn harvest had kept him driving the surrounding counties. Some farmers had endured rain, while other fields sat dry, waiting for the corn pickers and men.

As a result of all that driving, Sid had plenty of quiet time to think and pray about the future. With each day he felt more certain that God would honor his desire to pursue a future with Anna. Sid still didn't know what she would say—he hoped she'd say yes—but he knew he could ask.

He settled into the pew and tried to ignore the soft scent Anna wore and force his attention to the pastor. The sermon came from Hebrews 6, with the pastor focusing on anchoring to God. "Sometimes God asks us to follow Him without a clear plan or direction," the pastor explained, "but He will honor our faith."

Sid leaned forward, eager for that kind of bedrock faith. *Lord, I want to follow regardless of where You lead. Become my heart's true desire and passion. I want to trust and obey whatever You ask.* A settled feeling surrounded him. It would be hard to trust God that completely, but he'd learn. He knew he'd mess things up if left to his own devices.

No, he needed Someone bigger and wiser to direct his steps.

The service closed with another hymn, and all too soon, Sid stood in the aisle, looking down at Anna. Despite the week's setbacks, she seemed settled and calm. He liked the look. A lot.

"Will you join us at the farm for lunch?" Her eyes twinkled as if she knew he couldn't turn her down.

He toyed with the idea of saying no but discarded it. No,

he wanted to spend every moment he could with her. And once the new morning came, he'd be busy as ever, and she'd return to Kearney. "All right."

"Good. It'll be simple, but Papa can beat you at checkers to make up for that."

He followed them to the house, surprised by the lightness that filled the home. It was as if a heavy burden had lifted from it in the week since he'd stopped by. He watched Mr. Goodman closely and decided the root of the change came from him. The man walked and talked with a new freeness and openness. It seemed he'd wrestled with his demons and killed them. The change was far-reaching.

After a filling meal and a game of checkers, Sid grabbed Anna's hand and tugged her to him. She leaned into him, gazing at him with eyes filled with trust.

"Yes?"

"Let's go for a walk."

"The farm hasn't changed any in the last week, other than mud."

"Put on some boots, and let's stroll."

Anna raised an eyebrow at him then nodded. "I'll be right back." She returned a minute later having traded her church dress for a practical shirt, pants, and boots. He almost groaned at the change, except the shirt matched her cornflower blue eyes, making them sparkle even more.

He took her hand and pulled her out the door. Once outside, he tugged her out of sight behind the barn.

A mischievous twinkle filled her eyes. "What do you think you're doing, Specialist Chance? Stealing a kiss?"

He studied her sweet lips and liked the idea. "Maybe in a minute. First, I need to ask you something."

Anna leaned against the barn and waited. He loved the way she didn't rush to fill silence.

"I've thought a lot lately about us and what happens after the war ends." He rubbed a hand through his hair. Why was this so hard, even after rehearsing it continually on the drive to church and then to the farm? "What I'm trying to say is I love you, Anna Goodman. I love your heart. The way you fight to protect those who are important to you. The way you live life intently. And I want to share the future with you." He dragged his gaze to her face and groaned. Her mouth hung open, and she looked as though she'd just seen something horrible. "Maybe I will take that kiss."

He leaned closer, waited, saw her take a breath and collect herself. He eased nearer. "I love every single bit of you, Anna Goodman. Will you be my wife?"

She threw her arms around his neck and pulled him down until they stood eye to eye. "I will, Mr. Chance. But do not ever surprise me like that again." She closed her eyes. "Now you can kiss me."

❧

The next two months flew by for Anna. The harvest made it in, Papa settled back into farming, and they'd even received a couple of letters from Brent. Christmas Eve dawned bright and clear, with a thick layer of snow on the ground. Anna rolled over in bed, wanting to hold every moment tight.

"Come on, sleepyhead. Today's your day!" Dottie bounced up and down on her bed, already dressed in a beautiful suit. "If you don't hurry, we'll be late to the chapel." She sighed dramatically and threw her hand to her head. "I can't believe you get to use it before me."

Anna smiled. Guess she'd have to capture the moments as she lived them. Dottie wouldn't give her a moment's peace until she was dressed in her white suit. Then Dottie tried in vain to corral the curls around Anna's head, until Anna finally pushed her away.

"Sid wouldn't recognize me if you could restrain them." She took one last look in the mirror, touched up her lipstick, then grabbed Dottie's hand. "Let's go get Papa and head to the base."

Christmas Eve probably wasn't the best day to get married, but Sid had insisted he could imagine it no other way. She was the best gift he'd ever received, and he wanted to remember the day always. Fortunately, the chaplain had worked with them, squeezing thirty minutes into a day packed with services.

Papa stood at the bottom of the stairs, yanking on his tie. "Don't know why I have to wear this thing."

"Because your only daughter only gets married once. Don't be a bear on my day."

He grunted then helped her into her coat and the car. The Wisdoms had already left, and Anna couldn't wait to get to the church.

&

Sid paced the small foyer of the chapel. He tried not to look at his watch, but where was she? He'd waited almost an hour and hoped she hadn't changed her mind. Last night, she'd seemed sure before she shooed him away. Maybe he'd misread all the signs. What did he really know about women and serious commitments anyway?

"Calm down, soldier." Trent lounged against the wall, laughing at him. "She'll be here. You have to be patient. Isn't this what women do? Leave men waiting?"

"I suppose you're right. This is harder than I thought."

Trent pushed off the wall and straightened Sid's collar. "Don't worry. You look great. She'll be blissfully happy. And then you'll have to find a place to live in Holdrege."

"We'll be on the farm at least as long as I'm stationed at Camp Atlanta."

"Now that sounds like a recipe for newlywed bliss."

Sid socked Trent in the shoulder. "And what would you know about that?"

"Nothing." Trent looked toward the opening door. "But you'll know all about it very soon."

Dottie popped through the door, followed by Anna and her father. Sid's mouth dropped. Anna had never looked more beautiful than she did right now. Why had God chosen to bless him so? His heart slowly began to beat again, and he smiled at her.

"I'll let the chaplain know you're ready for him." Trent slipped into the sanctuary.

"Ready for this?" Sid whispered the words in Anna's ear.

"Absolutely." The promise of years together shone in her eyes.

Trent ran down the aisle. "The chaplain's waiting."

Sid smiled. He'd never been more ready for anything in his life. "Let's go."

epilogue

Sixty-three years later

Warmth flowed from the fire crackling in the fireplace. The laughter and pounding feet of children running up and down the stairs brought a smile to Anna's face. On those rare occasions when the whole family gathered, she couldn't help counting her blessings. God never ceased to overwhelm her with His goodness.

Since that day so long ago when Sid had taken her hand in the small white chapel at Camp Atlanta and they'd recited their vows, God had walked with them. Through the joys of the birth of each child. A daughter just like her. Two sons, each as different as could be. And a second daughter who brought deep joy to Anna's heart with the close friendship they shared.

But the story didn't stop there. No, by God's goodness, they'd walked through their share of valleys, always toward the hint of the sun's rays on the other side. They'd buried a child before his time. The company that employed Sid had layoffs. They faced uncertainty while he searched for his next job, and she returned to work long enough to make ends meet. Then there had been the loss of Papa and their eventual return to the farm.

Through it all, God had walked each step beside her. She'd even seen His hand prepare the way for them on occasion. How else could she explain the wonderful men and women who had joined their family by marrying the children? And the blessing when those unions added grandchildren to the family?

The grandchildren delighted her heart. They'd filled her

days with joy in her sixties as she chased seven little ones all over the farm. Now they'd magnified the joy by marrying and having children of their own.

Today the pounding feet that beat a rhythm in her heart came from the nine great-grandchildren. And next year, if God allowed her to live so long, there'd be two more. His goodness knew no bounds.

"What's putting that sweet smile on your face?"

Anna looked up. Sid stood beside her. Age had pushed his shoulders forward, and his knees didn't cooperate like they used to, but he was every bit the proud soldier she'd met in 1944. "Counting my many blessings."

He chuckled in a gravelly voice. "Let me guess. Four children and spouses, seven grandchildren and their spouses, and nine great-grandchildren."

"Yes. He's been so good to us."

Sid pulled her to her feet. "He has indeed. All right, everyone. Settle down for a moment."

Anna watched him, uncertain what Sid was up to as she snuggled into his shoulder. They hadn't discussed any grand announcements. But even after sixty-three years, he continued to surprise her.

The noise calmed down as their children and grandchildren found seats, while the great-grandchildren continued to play downstairs.

Sid cleared his throat. "Your mother and I agreed we wouldn't exchange gifts this year. When you reach our age, there's not much left that you need."

Soft chuckles filled the room.

"Sixty-three years ago, I first saw this lovely woman. She wore her blond curls in a short hairdo, and she had the perkiest nose and sweetest smile of any woman I'd ever seen. I decided then and there that I had to get to know her. Over the summer of 1944, she pushed me away, and then I pushed her away. We chased each other. Finally, I caught her, and I haven't regretted it for one moment. The white rose, please."

Anna's eyes widened as their oldest granddaughter, Catherine, came toward her with a single white rose. Tears pooled in the corners of her eyes when Sid took the rose and handed it to her.

"You were pure as this rose when we married. And the purity of our love has carried us through many years."

Anna buried her nose in the rose and inhaled its sweet fragrance, hoping to hide her emotion.

"But our love didn't stop in 1944. By God's immeasurable grace, our family has grown until we almost don't fit in this house anymore. Each addition to the family has been perfect. Each loss difficult. But through it all, my love for you never faltered. The red rose, please."

Catherine brought forward a single red rose. Sid took it and gently handed it to Anna. "Know that I have loved you for sixty-three years and will continue to love you for as many days and years as the good Lord chooses to give us."

He leaned toward her, hesitated. He wiped a tear from her cheek with a work-worn hand. Then he kissed her, and she responded from the depths of her soul. Loud whistles and applause filled the room until she pulled back from Sid.

"I love you, Sid."

"I love you, too."

She surveyed the room and knew that every moment, every challenge, had been worth it as she watched the evidence of their love.

A Letter To Our Readers

Dear Reader:

In order that we might better contribute to your reading enjoyment, we would appreciate your taking a few minutes to respond to the following questions. We welcome your comments and read each form and letter we receive. When completed, please return to the following:

Fiction Editor
Heartsong Presents
PO Box 719
Uhrichsville, Ohio 44683

1. Did you enjoy reading *Captive Dreams* by Cara C. Putman?
   ❑ Very much! I would like to see more books by this author!
   ❑ Moderately. I would have enjoyed it more if

   _____

   _____

   _____

2. Are you a member of **Heartsong Presents**? ❑ Yes ❑ No
   If no, where did you purchase this book? _____

   _____

3. How would you rate, on a scale from 1 (poor) to 5 (superior), the cover design? _____

4. On a scale from 1 (poor) to 10 (superior), please rate the following elements.

   ____ Heroine   ____ Plot
   ____ Hero   ____ Inspirational theme
   ____ Setting   ____ Secondary characters

5. These characters were special because? _____

_____

_____

6. How has this book inspired your life? _____

_____

_____

7. What settings would you like to see covered in future
   Heartsong Presents books? _____

_____

_____

8. What are some inspirational themes you would like to see
   treated in future books? _____

_____

_____

9. Would you be interested in reading other **Heartsong
   Presents** titles? ❏ Yes ❏ No

10. Please check your age range:

    ❏ Under 18   ❏ 18-24

    ❏ 25-34   ❏ 35-45

    ❏ 46-55   ❏ Over 55

Name_____

Occupation _____

Address _____

City, State, Zip_____

ALASKA
BRIDES

Three women have the strength needed to survive the Alaskan frontier and believe they don't need a man to achieve their goals. Can these women free their independant hearts to the power of love?

Historical, paperback, 352 pages, 5³/₁₆" x 8 "

Hearts♥ng

Any 12
Heartsong
Presents titles
for only
$27.00*

HISTORICAL ROMANCE IS CHEAPER BY THE DOZEN!

Buy any assortment of twelve
Heartsong Presents titles and save
25% off of the already discounted
price of $2.97 each!

*plus $4.00 shipping and handling per order
and sales tax where applicable.
If outside the U.S. please call
740-922-7280 for shipping charges.

HEARTSONG PRESENTS TITLES AVAILABLE NOW:

___HP571 *Bayou Fever*, K. Y'Barbo
___HP576 *Letters from the Enemy*, S. M. Warren
___HP579 *Grace*, L. Ford
___HP580 *Land of Promise*, C. Cox
___HP583 *Ramshackle Rose*, C. M. Hake
___HP584 *His Brother's Castoff*, L. N. Dooley
___HP587 *Lilly's Dream*, P. Darty
___HP588 *Torey's Prayer*, T. V. Bateman
___HP591 *Eliza*, M. Colvin
___HP592 *Refining Fire*, C. Cox
___HP599 *Double Deception*, L. Nelson Dooley
___HP600 *The Restoration*, C. M. Hake
___HP603 *A Whale of a Marriage*, D. Hunt
___HP604 *Irene*, L. Ford
___HP607 *Protecting Amy*, S. P. Davis
___HP608 *The Engagement*, K. Comeaux
___HP611 *Faithful Traitor*, J. Stengl
___HP612 *Michaela's Choice*, L. Harris
___HP615 *Gerda's Lawman*, L. N. Dooley
___HP616 *The Lady and the Cad*, T. H. Murray
___HP619 *Everlasting Hope*, T. V. Bateman
___HP620 *Basket of Secrets*, D. Hunt
___HP623 *A Place Called Home*, J. L. Barton
___HP624 *One Chance in a Million*, C. M. Hake
___HP627 *He Loves Me, He Loves Me Not*,
　　　　　　 R. Druten
___HP628 *Silent Heart*, B. Youree
___HP631 *Second Chance*, T. V. Bateman
___HP632 *Road to Forgiveness*, C. Cox
___HP635 *Hogtied*, L. A. Coleman
___HP636 *Renegade Husband*, D. Mills
___HP639 *Love's Denial*, T. H. Murray
___HP640 *Taking a Chance*, K. E. Hake
___HP643 *Escape to Sanctuary*, M. J. Conner
___HP644 *Making Amends*, J. L. Barton
___HP647 *Remember Me*, K. Comeaux

___HP648 *Last Chance*, C. M. Hake
___HP651 *Against the Tide*, R. Druten
___HP652 *A Love So Tender*, T. V. Batman
___HP655 *The Way Home*, M. Chapman
___HP656 *Pirate's Prize*, L. N. Dooley
___HP659 *Bayou Beginnings*, K. M. Y'Barbo
___HP660 *Hearts Twice Met*, F. Chrisman
___HP663 *Journeys*, T. H. Murray
___HP664 *Chance Adventure*, K. E. Hake
___HP667 *Sagebrush Christmas*, B. L. Etchison
___HP668 *Duel Love*, B. Youree
___HP671 *Sooner or Later*, V. McDonough
___HP672 *Chance of a Lifetime*, K. E. Hake
___HP675 *Bayou Secrets*, K. M. Y'Barbo
___HP676 *Beside Still Waters*, T. V. Bateman
___HP679 *Rose Kelly*, J. Spaeth
___HP680 *Rebecca's Heart*, L. Harris
___HP683 *A Gentlemen's Kiss*, K. Comeaux
___HP684 *Copper Sunrise*, C. Cox
___HP687 *The Ruse*, T. H. Murray
___HP688 *A Handful of Flowers*, C. M. Hake
___HP691 *Bayou Dreams*, K. M. Y'Barbo
___HP692 *The Oregon Escort*, S. P. Davis
___HP695 *Into the Deep*, L. Bliss
___HP696 *Bridal Veil*, C. M. Hake
___HP699 *Bittersweet Remembrance*, G. Fields
___HP700 *Where the River Flows*, I. Brand
___HP703 *Moving the Mountain*, Y. Lehman
___HP704 *No Buttons or Beaux*, C. M. Hake
___HP707 *Mariah's Hope*, M. J. Conner
___HP708 *The Prisoner's Wife*, S. P. Davis
___HP711 *A Gentle Fragrance*, P. Griffin
___HP712 *Spoke of Love*, C. M. Hake
___HP715 *Vera's Turn for Love*, T. H. Murray
___HP716 *Spinning Out of Control*,
　　　　　　 V. McDonough

(If ordering from this page, please remember to include it with the order form.)